Honey Pot Series

HONEY POT COLLECTION

Honey Pot Series

Ali Whippe

Honey Pot Series
Copyright © 2023-2024 Ali Whippe. All rights reserved.

Published By: 4 Horsemen Publications, Inc.

4 Horsemen Publications, Inc.
PO Box 417
Sylva, NC 28779
4horsemenpublications.com
info@4horsemenpublications.com

Cover by Nikki Tantillo
Typesetting by Valerie Willis

All rights to the work within are reserved to the author and publisher. No part of this publication may be reproduced, stored in a retrieval system, or transmitted in any form or by any means, electronic, mechanical, photocopying, recording, scanning, or otherwise, except as permitted under Section 107 or 108 of the 1976 International Copyright Act, without prior written permission except in brief quotations embodied in critical articles and reviews. Please contact either the Publisher or Author to gain permission.

All characters, organizations, and events portrayed in this novel are either products of the author's imagination or are used fictitiously.

All brands, quotes, and cited work respectfully belongs to the original rights holders and bear no affiliation to the authors or publisher.

Library of Congress Control Number: 2022951822

Paperback ISBN-13: 978-1-64450-779-7
Audiobook ISBN-13: 978-1-64450-781-0
Ebook ISBN-13: 978-1-64450-780-3

The Official Honey Pot Menu

Bound for Release

HONEY POT COLLECTION

Ali Whippe

Dedication

For all the boys I've topped before

Chapter One

MaryBell knows what James wants the moment she lays eyes on him. It is easy enough to see. A tall man, broad-shouldered with short black hair and those wire-rimmed glasses that remind her of John Lennon even after Harry Potter got a hold of them, James slowly makes his way over to her table. She knows the type: alone at a fetish event—but not in that creepy stalker way some of the attendees cultivate—rather, a not-quite-vanilla curious to explore some part of himself that wants something more. His will be a serious interest, not a passing thing, not a bet or a joke.

Looking over the array of strap-ons, dildos, and phallic objects on her table, MaryBell knows that her wares are often the victim of snickered hilarity, visitors jostling one another with wide eyes and goofy grins: "Hey, dude, I bet you could fit this up your ass!" and the quick retort, "You would know!" Such banter is common at the bigger conventions. She sets up her table under the harsh fluorescent lights of the vendor room and spends the day balanced between serious members of the community looking for new toys to add to their collections and curious onlookers who dare one another to go into the room and look at "those freaky toys"—and that is fine. MaryBell loves her work, loves being "that girl" at conventions, the one who can match wits over teasing jests just as easily as she can sit down and discuss the merits of one style of strap-on versus another. MaryBell knows her trade, knows it well, and she is always glad to have some fun, but she really likes when someone comes along who is genuinely interested in what she has to offer, someone who wants to try something new, but doesn't know where to begin.

Someone like James.

She is suddenly glad that she agreed to this gig tonight, knowing that the smaller venue and limited audience at the Fetish Night/ Dungeon Party at the Honey Pot instead of a local hotel means fewer people. The entrance fee for the event discourages the merely curious, allowing the well-versed members to have some fun in the dungeon set up nearby. MaryBell knows that her toys are harder to see in the relatively dim lighting, but the atmosphere encourages the attendees to act out scenes. To encourage them, the Honey Pot has a wide selection of BDSM equipment set up: spanking benches, St. Andrew's crosses, even a large metal cage large enough for a person to fit inside, hands bound to various points either above the head or at the waist. MaryBell hears the heavy thud of a leather paddle hitting flesh, and someone yelps and then moans. There are rules for playing at the event: no nudity, and no sex, but patrons are always happy to tie one another up and play with their toys—some brought from home and some purchased at the event.

It has been a good night, despite the smaller venue, but now that it is after midnight, things are winding down. Maybe after she packs up for the night in an hour or two, she might make her way over that way to the playroom. A few regulars tend to linger at the end of an event willing to perform one last scene. MaryBell doesn't think she will participate tonight, but she is always up for a bit of voyeurism.

Like watching the man who approaches her table now.

MaryBell lets her eyes linger on him as he walks up, taking in the details of his appearance in the dim light. He wears a green army jacket over a black t-shirt form fitting enough to see that he is in shape, but baggy enough to leave something to the imagination, and his jeans look comfortably worn. MaryBell decides she likes him. She doesn't move over to where he is though, knowing that someone with a serious interest will need time and space to take in the objects on her table on his own terms. When he is ready, he will come to her with his questions. She is content to wait, making a point to stand a little bit straighter though, improving her posture to accentuate her figure, just in case he cares to notice. She doesn't think he is gay, but sometimes she misreads these things.

James smiles briefly at her when he reaches the table, face open and friendly, not shy or embarrassed the way some patrons address her. She returns the look, but says nothing, watching as his eyes rove over the rows of plastic, rubber, hardwood, vinyl, and glass. He reaches out a curious hand to touch one of the glass dildos, fingers gently caressing the smooth surface, eyes creasing in surprised delight.

"It's a different sensation," MaryBell offers in a neutral tone, allowing him to decide if he wants to engage in conversation or just nod and move on.

"I imagine it would be cold," he says, picking up the piece and stroking it with his finger. "And it's so smooth. Can you even feel anything but the temperature?"

MaryBell nods, "Good point! Some people prefer that, though. It lets you focus on one sensation at a time." She reaches over to another glass dildo, this one purple and decorated with perfectly placed bumps and ridges. "This one has texture, so you get both the coolness and some friction and pressure." She hands it to him, noticing that he touches the tip of her fingers as he takes it, running his hands up and down the shaft as he nods.

"I can see that," he agrees. "But I don't know about that glass. I think I'd be paranoid about it breaking."

"Well, I'm not going to say it's impossible because anything can happen, but these are made to take a beating, and I've never heard of anyone actually breaking one, nevermind sustaining an injury."

He puts the dildo back down on the table, fingers touching the velvet tablecloth as he does so. "Well, as you say, anything is possible."

"Yes, it is." He looks up at her words, fully meeting her gaze, and she smiles, knowing that she is flirting, knowing that it is probably a bad idea to flirt with a curious newbie, but finding herself drawn to him. Smirking a little bit, she asks, "So, is there something I can help you with?"

He laughs, a smile reaching his eyes. "Maybe." He pauses, fingers trailing along the other pieces on the table between them. "I'm looking for something...different."

"Different how?" MaryBell asks, putting on her professional face.

"I'm not sure," he grins, then shakes his head. "Really helpful, I know."

"Well, let's start with the easy stuff. Is this something for you or your partner?"

This time his look is all flirtation. "I don't have a partner."

"Oh, well then. Your girlfriend then?" She tilts her head, making it clear she is joking.

He shakes his head. "Just me," he says, "and thank you for pointing out how lonely I am."

"I don't think someone like you is ever lonely," MaryBell tells him. "But are you...tired of the same old thing?"

James nods. "Exactly. If I want to try something else, what would you recommend?"

MaryBell considers him. "I think I need to know a little more about you first. Would that be okay?"

James nods.

"Let's start with your name."

"I'm James." He extends his hand to her. "And you are?"

"MaryBell," she replies, taking his hand and shaking it. It is a good grip, none of that ridiculous posturing and squeezing, but not cold and sweaty either. His touch is pleasant, and she doesn't want to let go. It has been a while since she felt such instant attraction to someone. It is refreshing. "And tell me, James," she says, flipping his hand over and examining the palm. His hand is big, but not huge, with long fingers. She feels the rough pads at the tips of his first and second finger, the classic mark of a guitar player, "Is this your first playtime or have you been here before?"

"Well, this definitely isn't my first time at the rodeo," he says, "but I've been thinking lately that I'd like to... get more involved." He lets her continue to hold his hand, watching as she runs her fingers across his palm. He looks up at her, his other hand reaching out to pick up one of her larger silicone dildos. "I want to *really* play this time."

She releases his hand and takes the toy from him. "Slow down there, cowboy. Even if this isn't your first rodeo, you'll need to ease into it." She puts back the extra-large toy and picks up a medium-sized one. She holds it up, showing him the features. "Wide base, so you don't lose it anywhere. It will actually suction cup to anything you stick it to, and it's made to fit a harness. Longer length, so it reaches the right places. A light layer of texture so you can feel some friction." At this, she takes his finger and runs it up and down the blue silicone. "And this one glows in the dark, so... bonus!"

"Does it actually glow in the dark?" he asks, curiosity mingling with surprise.

She nods. "Yep. Useful to find it, of course, but it's really cool to watch."

"So you've used this one before?"

"Well, not THAT specific one," she clarifies, then realizes that she is nearly blushing as she thinks about the last time she'd been with William. He really enjoyed that strap-on—she probably should have assumed he'd eventually decide to pursue relationships with men exclusively. "Apparently, it's pretty amazing," she pauses, then decides to just go for honesty. If James is anything like William, she'd rather know up front. "But I've heard it doesn't compare to the real thing." She waits for his reply.

"Well," James says slowly, "I think I will settle for pretty amazing then. I'm curious about the sensation, but I'm not that attracted to men, so I will pass on the real thing."

MaryBell cocks her head. "So, you are into women then?"

James nods. "Yes." It is a definite statement. MaryBell wouldn't mind if he is interested in playing with boys, but she wants him to want her as well, and she smiles at him, feeling the slow burn work its way up her neck, skin tingling as she thinks about how exciting it would be to play with a man like that again. William was a long time ago.

"Good." MaryBell pauses, debating if she is really going to do this. She isn't the type to randomly pick up a guy at an event and bring him home without getting to know him a little more first, but it has been a long time since she's been able to explore her dominant side, and James is definitely attractive. She looks him over again. He doesn't seem to be a crazed axe murderer type. *Then again, what does a crazed axe murderer look like?*

"Do you enjoy playing with toys like this?" James asks, distracting her.

MaryBell nods, "Oh yes. I love when I get the chance to use them." She pauses, then takes the plunge. "It's been a while since I've had that chance."

"Has it?" he asks, but it isn't really a question. "Huh." Now it is his turn to pause. She can practically see the thoughts spinning in his head, echoing her own. "Well, I haven't played with toys like this before, and I would love the chance to try them out."

MaryBell flushes, skin heating as she imagines him kneeling before her, hands bound and vulnerable, just begging her to fuck him. She shakes her head to clear it of the vision, deciding that she deserves this. It has been too long. But, first things first...she has bills to pay.

She points to the blue dildo in his hand. "Well, if you want to play with that toy, James, you're going to have to buy it first."

Chapter Two

Three hours later, MaryBell opens her front door to let James inside. "Hey," she says, still marveling that she has invited him back to her house after only knowing him a few hours. "You were able to find the place alright?"

"GPS got me here no problem," he replies, gesturing at his phone. "Can I park my car there?" MaryBell looks out the door at his red Nissan Sentra parked in her driveway behind her blue Mini Cooper. He is off the street, so no one will complain. Her neighbors can be a pain sometimes, but that is the price she pays for living in Hyde Park.

"Sure," she gestures for him to come inside. "But leave that phone on that table right there." She points at the side table near the front door. "No pictures. No videos."

"Of course not," James agrees, setting his phone down next to his keys. "Tonight, it's just us." She waits while he takes off his sneakers, leaving the Converse on the mat, and then his jacket, hooking it on one of the empty pegs by her front door. He pulls a package from the pocket as he hangs it up, handing the dildo to her without a word.

"Do you want anything?" she asks, taking his hand and leading him farther into the house. He takes in her simple decor, the black and white photos on the wall of the entryway, the black leather couch and Ikea TV cabinet in her living room as they make their way to her kitchen. MaryBell takes a seat across the hightop table from him, waiting as he settles onto the stool. She places the package at the edge of the table, ignoring it for the moment.

"I'm fine," he says.

"I know," she retorts, "and I can't wait to see how fine, but we need to talk about a few things first." James looks at her expectantly. "So," she begins, "let's talk about hard limits."

James smiles. "Well, like I say, this isn't my very first time, but I have limited experience. I'm not quite sure what my limits are."

MaryBell nods. "So are you okay with just telling me if I go too far? Or do you want to do the whole safe word thing?"

James shakes his head. "I'm not looking to play like that. I'm more curious about the sensation than the headspace."

"So this isn't about subspace tonight," she clarifies.

James shakes his head. "I mean, it's hot if you order me around, but it's not required. I like it, but I don't need it the entire time. You don't have to play a role or anything."

MaryBell nods again, taking his hand across the table and stroking his fingers. "Alright then. Anything else I should know about?"

James considers, face reddening as her fingers continue their slow massage. "So this is about you using that dildo on me, right?" He gestures at the package resting on the table. "How? Do you have a harness?"

MaryBell grins wickedly, letting her dominant side out a little bit. "Oh yes, cowboy. I won't just be pressing that into you with my hands. I'm going to fuck the bejesus out of you." James might not need to be submissive, but she definitely wants to dominate him.

James' quick intake of breath is encouraging, and she leans across the table, her hand caressing his face. "I'm going to grab those lovely hips, press you hard into the bed, and ride you until you scream your pleasure and beg me for more." MaryBell watches the heat rise in his neck at her words, and feels a responding pull in her lower belly. "So,

James," she says in a low voice, face close to his as she puts a knee up on the tabletop and scoots over to his side, "is there anything else we should discuss before we begin? Anything I should know about?"

"Are you going to tie me up?" James' voice is breathless, his eyes tracking from hers to her lips, only a few inches from his.

"I can," she says. "Would you like that, James? Do you want me to capture you and have my way with you?"

"Yes," he replies, and this time his eyes don't leave her lips. "Will you kiss me?"

"Oh yes," she says, moving her lips to his for a soft kiss. His lips are warm and inviting, tasting of the mint gum he must have chewed on the way over to her house. He waits for her to press her tongue into his mouth, allowing her to gently run her way along his teeth before meeting her with a soft press of his own tongue. MaryBell savors the feel of him, learning the rhythm of his kiss as she brings her body around on the tabletop, shifting from knees to sitting more solidly on her backside. She lets her hands roam over his neck and back, running her fingers through his hair, caressing his ears, pressing into the muscles of his neck and back. Her legs wrap around him, and he stands suddenly, carrying her off the table and spinning her around, pressing her against the wall.

"Ooh," she whispers against his lips, feeling the hardness of his erection through his jeans. "And I thought tonight was about me dominating you a little bit."

James chuckles, deep in his chest, hands holding her ass as he presses her into the wall. "Maybe I got a little distracted," he murmurs.

"Well, I'd hate for you to miss out on your new toy," she says, running her hands through his hair as she tightens her legs around his waist, letting the wall support her. "Though I definitely want to revisit this position next time."

He raises an eyebrow, but eases back, allowing her feet to touch the floor again. "Next time, huh? That sounds promising."

"Well," she says, hands reaching for his belt and pulling him toward her, "I suppose it depends on how the rest of the evening goes, but it's shaping up quite well so far." She unbuckles his belt, undoes his button, and unzips his fly, pushing his jeans to a heap on the floor. She glances down at the considerable bulge standing proud before her. "Quite well."

He looks at her, hands running down her arms to the bottom of her dress. "Can I undress you?"

"No," she tells him. "I'm undressing you tonight." She watches the excitement on his face he releases her, biting his lip as her hands move slowly down the dress, highlighting her curves as she moves to the bottom. She lifts it over her head in a smooth motion, feeling the rush as the air hits her skin, enjoying his eyes on her body.

She thanks the gods that she had decided to wear a matching bra and panties that morning, and smiles when he takes in her blue polka dots. They aren't ultra sexy, but they are definitely cute, and considering what she is about to do to him in a little bit, she thinks cutesy is a little bit funny. His hands reach out as if to touch her, but she reaches down, grabs them, and pushes them to his hips, making him wait. Then she reaches out and pulls his shirt over his head, revealing a chest that has some lines but not too much definition. She runs her palms down his skin, feeling the hardness of muscle, but not enough to turn him into a marble statue. She lets her nails trace little lines as she touches him, enjoying the small wince as she marks him gently.

"Now," she says in a tone that allows no opposition, "come with me." She steps to the table, grabs the package, and walks back to where he stands near the door, kicking his legs free of his jeans. She waits for him to finish, then grabs his cock through his shorts and begins leading him down the short hallway to her bedroom. James doesn't resist.

Her room has the same simplicity as the rest of her house: a queen-sized four poster bed, a small night table, and a dresser. She doesn't have a TV in her bedroom, but she does have a small speaker, and she contemplates putting on some music. *No*, she decides. *I want to hear every sound he makes.*

She leads him to the edge of the bed, then releases him, steps behind him, and pushes him onto the bed. He lands on his stomach, then crawls forward onto his knees. "Not yet, cowboy," she tells him, pulling him around to face her. "I get to play with you first. Sit here."

James does as he is bid, sitting on the edge of her bed, watching as she walks over to her dresser and opens the bottom drawer. She knows he can see the gleaming toys in there. She opens the package, slowly unwrapping the layers of paper and plastic that she always uses to wrap her customers' toys. She reveals the blue dildo, runs her fingers over its smooth surface, then sets the packaging aside. She checks to make sure that James is watching—of course he is watching, eyes wide with anticipation—and then she slams the base of the dildo down onto the top of her dresser, the wide suction cup immediately sticking to the surface, the soft glow barely visible in the dim light. It sways back and forth for a second before stilling.

James chuckles from his seat on her bed. "It really does glow!"

"It glows more if you let it soak up some light all day long," she admits. "This one has only been out for a little bit, so it's not very bright. But it will be next time."

She bends down slowly to her drawer, removing a cleaning wipe, and then slowly cleans the new toy, taking time to show James just how big it is. When it is shiny, she leaves it on the dresser, leaning down again to retrieve some simple restraints. She considers her options: the wide red and black cloth straps with Velcro seem the best choice for what she has in mind, though she eyes the purple bondage tape for a moment.

Nodding, she selects two of the cloth bundles, the hand ties wrapped up neatly into small circles. She ignores the matching foot restraints, knowing she won't need them tonight. She stands up, small bundles in hand, and walks over to him.

"You need to lay completely on the bed," she orders. "Head at the top, feet spread out." When James obeys, she kneels on his right side, first tying the open end of the restraint to the center of the headboard, and then wrapping the wide cloth cuff around his right wrist, making sure that the hold isn't too tight, but that the Velcro securing it around the outside is definitely in place. "Give that a tug," she tells him. When James does, his arm comes to an abrupt pause at the end of the tether, and it doesn't give it all. *Nice.*

MaryBell makes a slow show of crawling across his chest, then secures his other wrist to the next post over, so James lies with both hands directly above his head. She has considered spread-eagle, but she wants him on his belly at some point, and this way she can flip him over and over, and he won't get tangled up. The ties will just slip around one another, pulling him closer to the headboard, and that is fine.

Now that she has him at her mercy, she pauses to admire his body, kneeling at his left side as she takes in the lines of chest and hip, the straining erection pressing against his boxer shorts, the way his toes keep curling and uncurling in anticipation. She runs a hand down his chest, flicking his nipples as she does so, and watches the goosebumps rise on his skin. She leans down, blowing gently on each nipple, enjoying the gasp and sigh that her breath elicits.

He watches her intently, and she keeps eye contact as she moves down his body, pausing to breathe hot air against his straining cock through the fabric. His hips raise to meet her face, his eagerness pressing himself to her. "Hey now," she chastises, and his hips fall back into the bed, allowing her to move as she would. "Let's see you," she says, then slides the waistband of his shorts down, revealing a considerable shaft. She licks the tip, swirling her tongue around the sensitive head, and when he sucks in a breath, she draws him completely into her mouth, relishing the gasp that jerks from him. She sucks gently at first, moving slowly up and down the shaft, and when his hips relax, she pulls hard, enjoying the yelp followed by a satisfied groan.

She pulls back, sliding his shorts down his legs and off. She tosses them on the floor, then turns back to her bound lover, his eyes eager and excited. She knows he is probably debating the wisdom of his decision right now. He is curious to play, sure, but right now, he is falling back on old routines, and those habits want her to climb on top and ride him to orgasm. She can understand. That cock is impressive, and having him inside of her will be delicious.

But she wants a different kind of pleasure tonight.

She slides off the bed, taking the few slow steps to her dresser, knowing that he is watching her. She bends artfully to the bottom drawer, retrieving a bottle of lube, and then she stands and grabs the dildo from the dresser top. She makes a show of lubricating the length, hands sliding all around as she walks back to the bed, sure to have enough to spread everywhere. She crawls between his legs, then gently smacks his inner thighs until he raises his knees, giving her room to kneel between his legs. She pushes his legs out, asking him to tell her where is comfortable and where is too far. Making notes of the limits of his movement, she holds the dildo with one hand, then uses her other slick hand to rub his penis again, stroking him gently at first and then a little more roughly when he seems to relax, knees falling in toward where she sits.

As she slides her hand up and down his shaft, her other hand moves toward the sweet spot below his ball sac. She waits, then presses him there suddenly, loving the gasp that escapes him. She continues her slow up and down rhythm on his cock with her hand, while reaching lower with her other hand, this time spreading his butt and revealing the prize. She spreads some lube around, then reaches for the dildo, pressing the tip against him.

He shudders, his whole body tensing up. "Relax," she tells him, keeping up the rhythm with one hand and gently pressing with the dildo. He relaxes, and the dildo creeps forward an inch or so. She presses it slowly back and forth, gaining ground with each pass, but sure to listen to his breathing and feel his muscles to see when he needs her to pause.

"How's that?" she asks, when the dildo's head disappears into his body.

"Nice," he groans.

She slows her rhythm on his cock then, knowing that too much stimulation might cause him to come right there. William did, that first time. It took three separate tries before she actually got the special Rode-oh shorts on, strapped the dildo in place, and really fucked him before he came. Apparently, the sensation is overwhelming.

She presses the dildo deeper inside, easing into him, hand holding his dick with firm pressure but no motion. He presses down into her, clearly wanting more.

"Ready, are we?" she asks in a teasing voice, then pulls the dildo completely out of him, careful to place it on the bed where it won't roll onto the floor. He moans in disappointment. "Roll over," she orders. "Hands and knees."

As he obeys, she crosses to the dresser once more. She slides her polka dot panties off, replacing them with the pair of special shorts, and slides them up her hips, relishing the feel of the tight material pressing against her skin. She steps to the bed, knowing that James must be wondering what she is doing, enjoying the anticipation as it builds. She picks up the dildo, and slides it through the small circle cut into the front of the shorts. She presses it firmly into the ring of fabric meant to hold it in place, then presses it back against her, feeling the pressure against her clit.

This is going to be so awesome.

She considers adding the vibrator to the small pouch inside the special panties, but decides against it. She wants to feel herself pressing into him with each thrust. Vibration would help her come faster, sure, but she doesn't need the encouragement tonight. She is burning.

She picks up the lube again, running a bead along the length of the dildo one more time before she climbs on to the bed behind James. She presses against his legs until his knees are about shoulder width apart, then presses the tip of the dildo against his exposed flesh.

"Are you okay?" she asks, unable to read his expression because his face is pressed into the bed.

"Yes," he grunts. "So much more than okay."

"Good," she tells him. "Now tell me if it's too much. I will stop."

"Okay," he mumbles into the mattress, and then she feels him readjust his head, likely resting his forehead on top of his bound hands.

"Good boy," she says, unable to resist. She presses the dildo against him again, insistent this time, and then reaches around his hip with her right hand to rub his penis again. He is too large for her to easily reach the entire shaft, but she can reach enough to feel the hardness, the eagerness in him. She rubs him in a slow but determined rhythm, and then pushes the dildo inside him, just a little bit. He groans, and then tenses up. She waits, hand still stroking his cock, and he relaxes again. She pushes into him slowly, inch by inch, pausing as he needs, listening to his body, trying to ignore the slow burn of her own that grows each time she presses into him, the wide base of the dildo pressing hard against her clit. She wants to shove into him and start bouncing, rubbing herself against that hard surface, but she forces herself to wait, enjoying the slow temptation as she works inside him.

Soon enough, the dildo makes it beyond that place deep within him. She feels the ease of friction, and his whole body spasms against her. She thinks he has come, unable to help himself, but he moans, pressing his ass against her hips and gently wiggling back and forth, wanting more. She can feel the warmth of pre-cum on his dick, and she knows he won't last much longer.

But this is the fun part.

"You okay?"

"Mmm-hmm."

"Good." Without any warning, she withdraws and pushes back into him, pressing the length of the dildo deep inside, slipping past that sweet spot that elicits another moan. When he doesn't tighten up, but presses himself harder against her, she pulls back and dives in again, loving the pressure against her clit, feeling her own pleasure building, building.

"Oh fuck yes!" James yells as she draws back again.

"You like that, cowboy?" MaryBell asks, releasing his cock to place both hands on his hips, and yanks him back against her, relishing the pressure against her clit, that sweet feeling growing in her belly. "You like it when I fuck you?" She punctuates each word with another thrust, feeling his body buck in wild abandon. She is close now, so close, her hands digging into his hips with each push and pull.

"Oh yes!" he cries, and his whole body tenses up, orgasm flooding him. MaryBell thrusts into him two more times, her own orgasm wracking her body as she presses hard into him that last time. She collapses onto his back, pulse pounding in her fingertips, her hands still gripping his hips as if they are the only thing tethering her to the world.

For a moment, she is sure she will just float away if she lets go, but then the feeling passes, and she sits up, easing out of him as she backs away. She leaves him kneeling for a moment, letting him gather himself as she slips off the bed and out of the shorts. She places them in a pile on top of the dresser, knowing she will clean up later on.

James rolls slowly over, hands still bound over his head, face red with exertion, breathing heavily from his release.

"So," MaryBell says in her best customer service, "are you satisfied with your purchase tonight, James?"

James only moans in response.

Chapter Three

MaryBell sits in her car, wondering again why she has agreed to this. Just one date, James said. It will be fun, he cajoled, like dressing up and pretending to be a normal couple. She stares out the windshield at the sign at the edge of the parking lot: The Columbia. Of course, there is hardly anything more routine than a dinner date at the fanciest restaurant in Ybor City. The only way he could be more traditional would be if he'd taken her for steak at Bern's. By choosing The Columbia, he is being "different" and "exotic" in that way that all of these vanilla boys always think will excite the girls they pick up at the bar.

But they didn't meet at the bar. They met at a fetish club, and she came to terms with her sexuality a long time ago. It feels like a betrayal of sorts, to agree to come here and pretend to go on a "normal" date when all she really wants is to grab his hips and yank him back against her strap-on, feeling him tighten and hearing him moan in ways that she doesn't think any of those vanilla boys ever do during sex. She grins at the memory, unable to help herself. For a new boy toy, James is turning out to be way more fun than she anticipated. Even with ridiculous dinner dates, she knows that her playtime with him is only getting started.

She gives herself one more look in the rear view mirror before getting out of the car. She can play vanilla for a little while. Besides, she is always a sucker for good food.

The brief walk across the parking lot gives her a chance to adjust her dress, the baby blue material silky against her skin as she makes sure the back isn't riding up. She pulled out some lingerie for tonight, her garters buckled to the stockings at her thighs, her feet tucked into cute but comfortable low heels. If the wind doesn't gust, she shouldn't end up pulling a Marilyn Monroe on her way inside the restaurant. The air is humid, as always in Florida, but not the oppressive heat she knows is coming soon. She is trying hard to enjoy these last few days of relative coolness, imprinting the feeling in her memory to keep her steady during the sweat-soaked months ahead.

James already waits for her inside, looking sharp in his khakis and a button down shirt. He gives a little wave when he sees her, offering his arm as they approach the hostess.

Dinner is pleasant enough, filled with small getting-to-know-you topics like favorites and pastimes, past jobs and future plans, subtle and not-so-subtle flirtation, limits hard and soft, known and unknown, fingers touching on the table and some adventurous foot exploration under the table. MaryBell is glad that the tables have tablecloths, her stockinged feet completely hidden as she presses and rubs against James' crotch. When the server asks if they want dessert, she almost says yes, if only to prolong James' torture, but her belly is filled with delicious spiced meats and rice, and she doesn't want to eat anything else, especially knowing that the rest of the evening will likely be filled with vigorous activity.

They take a walk afterward, enjoying Ybor City at night, that magic hour right after the normal daytime shops have closed, but before the drunks and crazies really start living it up in the bars and clubs that line 7th Avenue. She points to the pizza shop across from the Ritz. "That place has the best pizza in Tampa," she declares. "Hands down."

He gestures at the cigar shop a few doors down. "This place has the best cigars in Tampa," he counters. "Hands down."

MaryBell looks at him. "You smoke?"

He shrugs. "Every now and then. I enjoy a good cigar with a whiskey." At her look, he adds, "Hey, I can be a stereotypical male sometimes."

"Not often," she comments, swatting his ass as they continue down the street.

"No," he agrees. "But I enjoy sensations. I want to try as many as I can."

When they reach the corner, he turns left, taking her hand as they walk slowly around the block and back in the direction of the parking lot where her car waits. It is quiet, the sun slowly disappearing behind the buildings, the everblue sky darkening to indigo when he pauses, steps closer to her, slowly easing them off the center of the sidewalk and over to the brick wall of the building. He presses against her, hands holding hers at her sides, looking at her with that slow smile, and then he kisses her, soft at first, but quickly building to something harder and more fierce. He pulls her wrists together in front of her body, holds them both with one hand, and then uses the other to rake through her hair, pulling the long dark tresses down from her perfectly messy bun.

MaryBell moans against his lips. When they pause for breath, she whispers, "I was hoping you would pin me up against a wall again, James."

"I'm glad to oblige," James replies, his hands leaving her hair to push both of her hands up above her head and against the wall. His hips press into her, and she braces her body weight on her left leg, lifting her right leg up to hook around him. His hands leave hers, roaming free over her shoulders, waist, and around the swell of her bottom. She feels him pause as he feels the hard line of the garter running down her thigh, and he breaks the kiss. "You came prepared."

"Always," she breathes. She wants more, to keep kissing him, rubbing against him, but they are standing outside in the street. Anyone could be watching.

The thought only excites her more.

She gives a furtive look around in the growing twilight. It isn't late enough for anyone to have stumbled onto 6th Avenue yet. People walking here will have a specific destination. MaryBell doesn't see anyone. She gives James a delightfully wicked look, and then glances again from side to side.

No one walks. No cars move on the brick-lined street. There are a few cars parked on the street, but no one seems in a hurry to get into them. They are fairly hidden against the wall, standing as they are underneath an overhang, tucked between two doors that are probably employee exits. She doesn't see any telltale cigarette butts near the doors though; it is unlikely that any employees would come bursting outside for a smoke break.

James makes the same surveillance, hands never leaving her body, feeling her butt through the silky material of her dress, then skirting beneath to caress her bare skin. "Naughty girl," he murmurs, deft fingers stroking the damp center between her legs. She presses closer to him, her leg wrapping hard around his lower leg, trying to not be so incredibly obvious if someone does happen to walk by. His hand continues to press, fingers moving slowly back and forth, building the heat within her. When she moans, he kisses her, swallowing the sound as he moves his lips in concert with his fingers. She can feel the press of his erection, but at the moment, she doesn't care. All that matters are those fingers pressing, rubbing, caressing, and his mouth on hers.

"Yes," she says into his mouth, "dear god James like that yes!"

As the orgasm spills through her, her muscles lock, the rushing wave paralyzing her, and then she sags, boneless, and James holds her upright as she shudders with the force of her release.

When she thinks she can stand without difficulty, MaryBell puts her foot down and leans against the wall. James pulls away, face suffused with pleasure. "That was fun," he says, offering her his hand as he steps back, glancing quickly up and down the street, noting again that they are still alone. "I've always wanted to do that."

"What? Make out on 6th Avenue?" MaryBell is still a little breathless, but she takes his hand and starts slowly down the street back to the parking lot.

"Well, sure, but really, I always wanted to make a woman come in public, not sure if we would get caught." He pauses, grinning at her, then pulls her hand up to his lips and kisses it. "And thank you, MaryBell, for being so prepared."

"There is something to be said for old school lingerie," she admits, "but I always find panties to be a nuisance."

He nods, and they continue walking, both of them glowing with satisfaction of a night well begun, but not yet finished, each knowing that even more pleasures awaits.

Chapter Four

MaryBell follows James to his condo in one of the high-rise buildings on Channelside, leaving her car in the visitor spot when he parks in his assigned space. He walks with her through the well-lit garage to the elevator, holding hands as they wait for it to arrive. When they step inside, MaryBell looks at the numbers on the panel. "What floor?"

"20." He taps the button, and the elevator begins to rise smoothly.

"Is that the penthouse?" she asks, smiling at him.

"No," he says, pulling her to him for a kiss. "Are you sorry I'm not that kind of guy?"

MaryBell returns the kiss, feeling the heat begin to build in her belly again. "No," she says. "I like you as you are, James. I don't need a penthouse to make me like you more." She kisses him again, then pulls away to laugh, "Of course, on the 20th floor, I'm expecting an amazing view."

"That I do have," he replies, hands tugging at her hair. "I have a balcony, too, and I can't wait to have you out there, bare ass naked, pressed against the railing, all of this glorious hair blowing free in the wind."

MaryBell moans, arms reaching around him, hands tugging his shirt out of his pants so her fingers can skate up his back and rake him with her nails. The elevator arrives, and they pull apart, stepping out into a short hallway done in neutral beige. There is a table with fresh flowers in a vase set across from the elevator.

Noticing MaryBell's curious glance at the flowers, James says, "It's the condo association. They maintain the hallways, deal with the garbage, and make sure every floor has fresh flowers. You know, the important things."

"Do you get room service, too?" MaryBell jokes.

James grins. "Not quite, but there are quite a few places who deliver here." He assumes a serious air. "You do know that Channelside is *the* up-and-coming neighborhood in Tampa, of course?"

"Of course," she replies in the same tone, "and the view from that balcony better be amazing for the price of this 'up-and-coming' neighborhood. I remember when the only thing here was the arena and the aquarium."

"Me too. I was lucky enough to get in at the start, back when there were only a few buildings and a lot of hope and promises."

"Nicely done," she compliments him as they approach his doorway. "Are you always so good at spying an opening?"

James turns to grin at her as he turns the key in his front door with a look that is all male. "Sometimes."

MaryBell smiles back at him, then pushes him into the condo as the door opens. He turns to face her, using his momentum to drag her in behind him, foot kicking the door shut behind them. "Now," he tells her, "it's my turn."

MaryBell shivers in anticipation, then pauses to consider the entryway. "Do I get a tour first?" she asks in a low innocent voice.

"But of course," James replies, "but I won't lead you around by your dick."

"That's only because I didn't bring my toys tonight."

"No worries. I have some of my own." He waves for her to follow. "Welcome to my lovely home," he grins, leading her into the open plan living room and kitchen. "Bathroom behind you," he points to a door in the wall behind her, "but the bigger one is off the master." He gestures at the glass doors on the far side of the room, "The fabled balcony which you will certainly see later." He leads her down a small hallway off to the right, "Bedroom is right here." MaryBell glances inside to see a bed with a metal headboard, but he doesn't go in. "And this is my office." He steps inside, and MaryBell follows, taking in the desk and chair, but completely impressed by the wall of windows overlooking the Hillsborough River and the port.

She walks over to the windows, placing a hand against the cool glass, "You work from home?"

James walks up behind her. "Yup," he says, kissing her neck and pulling at the tie that holds her hair in place. She fixed the bun during the short drive over here, but she knows it is a lost cause. He tugs it free, and her hair spills down her back. "Finally," he breathes. "I've wanted to do that since we first met."

"Play with my hair?" she asks, pressing her hips back against him. "Is that what you've been longing for, James?"

He spins her around to face him. "Among other things, but I think we've already played with walls tonight." He takes her hand, and then motions for her to sit in the desk chair. It is surprisingly comfortable, she notes, with perfect lower back support and a high back for her head to lean against.

"This is a nice chair," she observes, hands pressing into the armrests.

"It better be," he says. "I spend a lot of my time sitting in it." He pauses, and then reaches into a small bin tucked underneath the desk. "And the next time I do, I want to think of you sitting in it." He reaches into the bin, pulling out black restraints, a wide cuff with Velcro on the outside attached to a long strap meant to be tied to anything. "Now," he orders, in a tone that sends thrills through her belly, "take off your dress."

MaryBell scoots the silky material out from under her butt, and then slips it over her head, tossing it on top of the closed laptop that rests on the desk. She leans back into the chair, spreading her legs, stockings and garters matching the simple pattern of her bra. She looks down at herself. "Anything else," she pauses, then adds, "Master?"

He chuckles, but seems to consider. He idly flips the restraints against one palm as he stands. "Your bra," he says. "How much do you like it?"

Now it is MaryBell's turn to consider him. "Why do you ask?"

He reaches for her hand, and she gives it to him, face curious. He secures the cuff around her wrist, making sure the Velcro is tight but not uncomfortable. "How's that?" He lets her ponder as he cuffs the other wrist. With the restraints around both wrists, MaryBell takes a moment to touch each one with her still mobile hands, checking the tension against her skin. Finding it bearable, she nods, and then James yanks on the ends of the restraints, first lifting her hands out in front of her with a grin, then tugging them down and to her sides as he spreads his arms wide. Standing up, he moves around behind the chair, keeping the tension on the straps as he secures them, tucking her hands next to her waist, firm against the back of the chair.

"Is this a favorite bra?" he asks again from behind her now, giving her some slack in the ties, but only enough to rest her hands next to her butt. It isn't tight enough to pull her shoulders oddly though. She is quite comfortable.

"No," she admits, speaking over her shoulder to where he kneels, securing the straps. "It's pretty generic, to be honest. I got the beige to match the garter, really, and those I do love."

"Noted," James says, standing up behind her and spinning the chair to face him. "So," he begins in a low voice, one hand reaching behind the chair to grab something off the desk, "you wouldn't mind if I," he pauses, pulling the pair of scissors in front of her, "cut it off?"

MaryBell gapes at him. They discussed limits over dinner, but this hasn't come up. She considers it, deciding that the very idea of him cutting her bra off her while she sits tied to his chair is thrilling. "No," she tells him, "I wouldn't mind."

"Good," he says, pressing the scissors under one strap. The cool metal makes her shiver, and then he snips the material. The strap falls down, and gravity goes to work almost immediately. MaryBell has large breasts, and without the support, her right breast relaxes. She looks down at it, and then at him. He reaches out, pushes the cup underneath to free her skin, and puts his mouth on her nipple. MaryBell sighs at the warm rush of his lips. His hands hold her waist, then run down her legs, tracing the line of the garters from her hips to her thighs. He keeps his mouth on her nipple, sucking harder and then softer, alternating rhythm, and she wants to press his head against her. She reaches out, but her hands stop at the end of the restraints, fingers straining uselessly against her sides. He releases her nipple, and then retrieves the scissors from where he has abandoned them on the floor. He runs the cool metal across the sensitive skin of her collarbone, and then snips the other strap. Her bra folds down, but instead of tucking it under as he has her first breast, he uses the scissors once more in the middle, then pushes the bra aside, hands caressing her bare skin.

James kisses her breasts, then scoots down, rolling the chair closer to where he kneels, and pushes her back into a reclined position. The chair leans back in that terrifying way for a moment, and MaryBell gasps, but then she hears a click as the chair locks into position, and she relaxes, looking down her body at James' dark head now poised above her middle.

He looks up at her, eyes dark with anticipation. "You want me to touch you?"

MaryBell nods, straining to raise her body to meet him, but her hands keep her tethered to the chair.

James traces a line down her belly, then runs his hand between her legs and slips into her wetness. "You want me here?" His fingers are quick, rubbing against her clit in the way he knows she likes.

"Yes," she moans.

James slips a finger down, sliding inside of her. MaryBell strains harder, trying to press her hips against him. "You like me inside you?"

"God yes!" she says, as he begins to move his finger in and out in a teasing rhythm. James uses his free hand to lift one leg over his shoulder and then the other, and then bends to lick her, tongue warm and demanding against her secret flesh, his other hand never pausing in the rhythm. James knows his business, and the combination of sucking and licking with his finger inside has her shuddering within moments. She longs for her hands, wanting to press his head into her body, wanting the feeling to never stop, and then the wave rushes over her, and she quivers in the chair, body going limp as the orgasm crests and then fades. James lifts his head, resting his cheek against her thigh. "I love how you look right after you come."

MaryBell focuses on catching her breath, enjoying the support of the chair as she floats back down from the euphoria of the orgasm. James moves away from her, lifts the chair upright, and spins her so he kneels behind her. She feels him untie the restraints, and then he spins the chair again, pulling the ties around in front of her, and then he stands up, tugging her after him, using the restraints as a guide. "I believe I promised you a lovely view," he says, leading her out of the room on shaky legs. She follows, and when James opens the balcony door, she shivers as the cool air brushes her naked skin.

The balcony runs the length of the room, but MaryBell sees that James only has a table and one chair outside. She looks out into the night sky, realizing that she can see the boats in the port across the river, but it is unlikely that anyone could see them up here, since they are so high off the ground. She looks at the chest high railing and then at James, eyebrow quirked.

"It's sturdy," he says. "Trust me."

"I do," she says, watching as he lets go of her restraints long enough to remove his shirt and kick off his pants. His erection is a huge bulge in his boxers, and MaryBell's belly tingles, eager to feel him inside of her. "So," she says, standing before him in only her garters and stockings, hands cuffed, but the tethers trailing on the floor in front of her. "Where do you want me?"

James walks toward her, picking up the restraints and using them to pull her closer to him. "Well, I think I want you outside on the balcony, all that glorious hair running riot down your back while I fuck you from behind..." He pauses, then grins. "But I want to see your face this time, so maybe we'll keep that for later."

MaryBell feels an answering smile on her own face. "So...?"

He gestures at the table. "Hop up."

She does, gasping as the cold table top hits her bare skin, spreading her legs where she perches on the edge. James steps out of his shorts, his cock hard in the moonlight as he puts the condom on, and MaryBell reaches a hand to touch him, only to have James use the restraints to pull her hand away.

"Oh no," he tells her with a playful smirk. "Tonight is my night to play."

MaryBell puts both hands down at her sides, smiling innocently at him. "I only want..." she lets the words trail off, wanting to keep the game going.

"I know what you want," he says, stepping right in front of her, cock pressed against her opening, but gentle, so gentle. She longs to scoot forward, to feel all of that hard length inside of her, but she stops herself. "You want to pull me into you, want to ride my cock, want to come again and again."

"Well, yes," she admits, skin flushed with anticipation as the tip of his cock teases her, presses hard against her but does not move. "I do want to do that, but right now, I just want you to fuck me."

His hands find the restraints, wrapping the tethers around and tugging her hands behind her back while moving her toward him a fraction of an inch, and all that hardness is touching her now, her skin aching for him to move, to push into her, but he holds himself firm. "Look at me," he urges, and she tilts her head back, eyes looking into his as he wraps one arm around her back and the other grabs her hip. She can feel the restraints pressing into her skin as he pulls her hands tighter behind her back, but it is a delicious feeling. If her hands were free, she would be climbing him by now, forcing her pleasure even while he wanted to linger in the moment. His cock moves another fraction closer, and she feels her skin pull around him as he stretches her. She aches for more, her whole body trying to press into him.

"Wait for it," he tells her, eyes never leaving hers as he creeps inside of her. "You naughty little vixen," he purrs, giving her another small motion. He is inside of her now, but barely, just the tip, her skin screaming for more. "You need to learn some patience," he says, smiling as he gives her yet another inch. "You spend so much time ordering people around, having your way with them when you want it, as you want it," and here he pulls out a little bit, eliciting a moan of frustration from MaryBell. She squirms, trying to get that precious inch back, but he holds her tight. "You need to learn to slow down," he urges, and then he moves forward again, teasing her with his cock slowly, each movement a torrent of tortured delight. She groans when he makes it halfway, relishing in the fullness of him, sensitive skin thrilling at each slight movement. She closes her eyes then, bites her lip, and looks at him with pleading eyes.

"Please," she begs. "Please fuck me."

James gives her another inch, and then pauses. "I am fucking you," he tells her.

"More," she moans. "I need more."

"Do you?" he asks, and then with a swift moment, he sheaths himself to the core. MaryBell screams with the sudden ferocity, and her head falls back. But then James' hand is in her hair, yanking her face back up to see his. He draws back and plunges into her again, and MaryBell's body shivers, the combination of sensation and the cool air almost sending her right over the edge into another orgasm. "Yes!" she yells, and then James' mouth is on hers, tongue demanding as he moves against her again, body hard as he fills her. MaryBell wraps her legs around his hips, urging him on to greater speeds, and almost immediately, he stops moving, cock barely inside of her. She opens eyes that she hasn't realized she has closed to look at him.

"Oh no," he tells her. "You don't get to set the rhythm this time." He waits, then plunges in and out of her, hovering just outside. "This time," and he begins the long, slow push inside again, "you are at my mercy."

MaryBell lets her legs fall from his hips, willing herself not to move, relishing the feel of him pressing into her with long, slow strokes. She can feel her orgasm building, knows that if he moves just like that for a few more seconds, she will come, the wave crashing over her in a daze.

"Please," she whispers against his mouth, loving how his hand tangles itself in her hair at the base of her neck, his other hand pressed tight against her hip with the restraints pulled taut across her lower back.

He pulls away just enough to see her face. "Please what?"

"Please fuck me," she pauses a moment, then adds, "Master."

He moves faster into her at the word, hips pressing hard. "What was that?" he asks, though he has clearly heard her.

"Please fuck me, Master!" she yells, and he buries his head in her neck, mouth sucking at the skin above her collarbone as he begins to pound into her in earnest. The table begins to rock dangerously, and he lifts her, abandoning the restraints so the straps fall free. Her legs wrap hard against him as he spins, pressing her against the concrete wall next to the balcony doors and fucking her with such force that she begins to come almost immediately. She slides her hands around his neck, restraints forgotten in the sudden passion, and kisses him, reveling in the total wild abandon of the moment. She cries out her pleasure, biting James' shoulder in her excitement, and he drives himself into her two more times before his body shudders. He holds her up for another moment, both of them breathing heavily, and then his arms shake alarmingly, and they both slide down the wall, her legs releasing his waist as they sit on the balcony floor.

MaryBell laughs breathlessly. "And I thought you said we were done with walls for one night."

James shrugs, chest heaving as he catches his breath, then reaches for her wrists to release the restraints. "I guess I got excited."

MaryBell catches his face with her newly freed hand. "I like it when you get excited." She leans forward to kiss him, this time slow and gentle, a kiss just for fun, not leading anywhere.

When they separate, James finds his feet and stands up, then offers his hand to lift her up. They go back inside, James wandering into the kitchen and opening the fridge. He comes back to hand her a bottle of water.

She takes it gratefully, taking a swig and sighing. "So, James," she says, "are we going to do this again sometime?"

"I hope so," he says. "I expect you to bring your strap-on."

Fetish Circuit

HONEY POT COLLECTION

Ali Whippe

Dedication

For all the boys seeking a Mistress

Chapter One

"So, you like to watch, do you?" Katie's voice is a low thrum, and Steve doesn't remember her sounding quite so sultry from their days together back in high school.

Hell, did I ever really listen to her back then at all? Probably not.

She certainly didn't have those amazing tits when she was his partner in his science class. Those breasts are largely to blame for this meeting, that short exchange at the reunion leading to the inevitable "We should hang out sometime" to "catch up on each other's lives."

He'd meant he could catch up on some quality time checking out her lovely shape beneath that shirt. He'd been pleasantly surprised when she accepted so readily, but happy at the chance to see her again somewhere beyond the dim lights of the special events room at the Tampa Hyatt.

He likes looking at her.

He likes the way she doesn't blush or look away from him, even though she must know he has spent most of the conversation marveling over the pale curve of cleavage peeking up out of her plain black button down shirt.

Did she even have tits when I sat next to her in high school?

He doesn't remember. Maybe these are fake. Steve has certainly had his hands around several pairs that were in the last ten years. It is a mystery he suddenly wants to solve, and he takes a moment to shift in his seat to accommodate the slight swelling in his pants.

The girl knows how to dress to highlight her attributes. Her jeans are just tight enough to outline an ass in desperate need of smacking, but not tight enough to make him wonder how she is breathing in them. The shirt is blessed with a neckline low enough for him to contemplate that slow tease of cleavage again, though not as low cut as her black dress the night before had been. He tries to stare at her chest only when she isn't looking at him, which turns out to be not very often.

Katie has grown bold over the years, and her gaze rarely leaves his as she speaks, almost daring his eyes to wander. So far, he has only stumbled that way twice, both times returning guiltily to her knowing smirk. The second time, she stopped what she was saying—something about college—grinned a wicked grin he had never expected to see on her face, and put one hand under his chin, tugging it down so her chest filled his entire view while her other hand pulled down her shirt front just far enough for him to glimpse something red and satin and way too lacy to be a regular bra. Before he even registered what she had done, she had released his chin and her shirt was back in place. For a second, he wondered if he was fantasizing, but then she had followed it up with, "So, you like to watch, do you?"

"Umm..." he stutters, suddenly off balance as he has not been in years. "No!" He pauses, still looking at those demanding eyes. Then he shrugs, giving it up. "Well, yeah," then he adds, "but who doesn't, Katie?"

"It's Katharine now. I haven't been Katie in years," she laughs, a low purr in her throat that is definitely not part of the girl he remembers. "Watching can be entertaining," the woman across from him says, "if the show is worthwhile."

"Show?" he sputters. "Is that what they teach you in that school of yours?" She had told him of her latest grant-funded research at the local university, Abraxus Tasker College.

"No," she replies quite seriously, "those kinds of shows are not academic in any way." She pauses long enough for him to take in what she has said, then adds, "I don't have a degree in voyeurism after all."

"No," he agrees. "Chemistry you said."

Her eyebrow quirks. "You were listening?"

He leans into the table, closer to her. "I always listen."

"But do you obey?"

The question takes him off guard, a little too close to home for comfort. "What?"

"If you listen so well, do you take direction as well? Can you obey?"

This is not a conversation he ever imagined having with Katie—Katharine—the little nerd who had made sure he passed with an A. "What do you mean: obey?"

Her hand darts across the table to land on top of his, pinning it to the smooth wood. He instinctively tries to jerk away, but she barks at him, a short, sharp "No!" that somehow manages to be swallowed by the swells of the conversations around them. His hand freezes in place, and his cock hardens at once. He stares at her.

How does she know? He thinks of the small pile of satin panties hidden under his bathing suits, the secret delight of wearing women's clothes.

She looks at him for a long time, then says, "Don't move" in that same firm voice that makes him swell even more. He sits still, his hand pressed hard against the table top, chest suddenly very full of something he can't explain.

Her lips curl into a wicked grin to match the one he saw earlier, and she says, "You do take direction. Well done." When Steve continues to stare at her, blank faced and stone still, she takes a long sip of her coffee, chuckles, and says, "You are allowed to talk, you know."

"What are you?" Steve breathes, his hand itching to move, to slide closer to her across the table, but he forces it to stay there, a slow tease between desire and action that makes him want to adjust on the cheap plastic seat. He refuses the urge, sitting perfectly still.

Katharine shrugs confidently. "I'm a scientist," she says casually, then adds, "You may move now too."

Steve is amazed to feel his body relaxing, as if her voice has given him permission to release something held too tightly. For a second, his vision swirls as he lets it go, then he shuffles in his chair, hands coming together around the fading heat of his coffee cup. What has she just done to him? "You know what I mean," he says. "That voice!"

"My voice?" she asks innocently, coy now. "What do you mean?"

"You just... were so.... demanding," he manages, trying to focus around the sudden hope dawning in his chest. Would she do it to him again?

She shakes her head. "Not me," she says. "You're just in dire need of topping. I bet you'd fold for anybody right now."

"Topping?" he asks, trying to place the word beyond the ice cream context his brain has suddenly decided to play out before him—a vision involving chocolate syrup and Katharine's mouth that forces him to shift again in his chair. "What's that?"

She laughs a little. "You're not serious, are you?" When he doesn't reply, brain caught between his growing erection and the image of Katharine's mouth, shiny with chocolate, she stops laughing. "Wait, are you serious?"

"About what?"

"About not knowing what topping means."

"Ice cream?" he tries.

She shakes her head at him, eyes quirking. "Have you really lived this long without acting on this?"

Steve is suddenly suspicious of where this conversation is heading. "Acting on what?"

"You're a sub, Steve. You always have been."

"Sub? Like a teacher?"

She takes a deep breath now, as if trying to accept his level of confusion. "No, like a submissive."

"What do you mean?" *She can't really be saying this out loud,* Steve thinks.

She moves slowly, her hand coming across the table and resting gently on top of his. "You've never had anyone top you before, have you?"

"Tup me?" he shakes his head. "I'm not really into that, if that's what you mean..."

"*Top* you," she says, fingers tightening between his, carefully enunciating the word. "Dominate you."

Steve considers pulling his hands back into his lap, but that feeling in his belly is back again, and he restrains himself. Still, something about that isn't right, so he pushes a little against her grip. Her fingers tighten in reflex and suddenly it hurts a little. He imagines her knuckles must be white, straining as she is to keep him inside her grip, but now, now that little glow is right, the promise of something that could grow.

"I've been dominated," he is saying. "My ex always had to be in charge."

"That's not what I mean, and I think you know it," she tells him, hands squeezing for a second even harder, and the bright pain blossoms for an instant and then is gone, replaced by something disturbingly close to ecstasy. The words burn in his mind, and for a second, he doesn't say them, doesn't let them pass his lips, but then she is giving him that look again, that look that will not be denied, and he hears himself speaking so quietly that she probably can't even hear him.

"Please tell me what you mean, Mistress." Apparently, she can hear him because her hands leave his at once, the space where they had been both relieved and missing that sturdy, confident pressure.

He wants to flex but refuses, relishing the feeling as needles promise to replace numbness.

"I thought so," she says. "How long has it been for you?"

He doesn't want to tell her, is embarrassed and curious and excited and angry all at once, but the words come out anyway, the need to please her suddenly overwhelming everything else. "Never," he mumbles, then says it again, more loudly, "Never the way I wanted it."

She leans closer to him, relieving him of the burden of speaking out loud, her voice an intimate whisper of control and understanding. "How do you want it?"

"I want it to be real," he admits, astonished to find the words coming so easily, but aware that they have been inside a long time, just waiting for the right person to conjure them forth. "I want to not have to be in control and to have the girl for once really take charge and mean it."

She smiles at him then, a long slow smile that reminds him of how uncomfortable his boxer shorts can get sometimes. "You really want someone to take charge of you, Steven?"

He nods.

"Say it," she says sharply, yet still in that same intimate voice, and he manages to speak.

"Yes, Mistress."

"Well, then," Katharine says, clearly considering. "If you really want to do this, come to my apartment at 9 tomorrow night. Right at 9," she repeats, "and not a minute later, and we'll see what we can do."

"Do..." Steve echoes, then his brain kicks back on, and he asks, timidly, "Will you have sex with me?"

"Maybe," Katharine says in that same almost sweet, not to be argued with voice. "Maybe not."

"Then what will we do?" He is coming out of that sweet feeling now, coming back into his head and his body, a slide that has him both relieved and annoyed at the same time. His cock aches, then starts to subside, that growing sensation in his gut fading as Katharine leans away from him.

"Then," she replies in a normal voice, "you will have the genuine experience you are craving."

Steve is nodding, knowing that this is what he wants but uncertain of how to proceed. "Should... should I bring protection?" he asks, thoughts mingling with a growing excitement in his mind.

Katharine shakes her head. "You're missing the point," she tells him. "This is about more than sex. This is about easing that ache in your belly. That I can certainly do for you."

"You think so?"

"I know so," Katharine says quite confidently, then her voice changes again, and she is serious now, business-like. "We should probably establish some ground rules before we begin..."

Chapter Two

Steve stands near the elevator, wrist held out before him, checking his watch. 8:57. Three more minutes. He knows that it will take him less than a minute to walk down the hall, turn the corner, and find himself standing in front of her door. He checked. Her apartment is J, the one all the way at the end, the corner unit. She shares only one wall with K. Steve wonders if she chose the apartment because of that. She could probably make a lot of noise before anyone would hear it, especially if she was in the rooms far away from that one shared wall.

Steve is very aware of neighbors, knowing just how thin some walls can be. He's spent enough nights listening to all of his neighbors going about their lives. Katie—Katharine he reminds himself again—lives in a nicer building by far with much thicker walls. Chemistry must pay well.

He glances at his watch again. 8:58. He takes a moment to check his appearance in the mirror across from the elevators. His hair is fine, short enough to be respectable but not severe. His shirt is simple, button down black hiding the white tank top he wears beneath. He's not sure why he still wears undershirts, but his father always had, and so Steve still does. He appreciates the extra layer during the harsh winters, though the summers always make him contemplate a change. The pants are plain khakis, and he can either dress up or down depending on whether he tucks in his shirt to reveal his belt. He's wearing loafers to complete the look, comfortable but not quite sneakers.

He checks his teeth in the mirror, sniffs his breath, and then peeks at his watch again. 8:59. It's time.

He takes the few steps down the hallway, heart speeding up as he turns the corner, knowing that this time he gets to knock, gets to enter, and then gets to experience...whatever Katharine has in store.

9:00.

He knocks on the door, two hard raps. The door opens inward to reveal a long hallway lined with tasteful paintings. A voice says, "Come in."

Steve steps inside, eyes adjusting to the dimmer light as the door shuts quietly behind him. He turns around to see Katharine flicking the locks with a practiced hand before she turns to lean casually against the locked door. Her gaze doesn't leave his.

Steve tries to keep his eyes on her face as she clearly expects him to do, but he can't help himself from trailing down from that still-so-familiar face, the long unbound dark hair and bright eyes, to the tight blue tank top that reveals a delightful swatch of considerable cleavage, the short black skirt brushing up against the lace tops of black stockings. He thinks she may even have garters holding them up. His eyes leave her thighs and slide down the rest of her to the floor and her feet, one flat on the floor, the other pressed back against the door. His gaze lingers on her feet for a moment. He expected high heels or boots or something, but the idea of those stockinged feet touching his skin, running along him, is enticing.

"You're on time," she says. "Well done." Steve is about to reply, but she cuts him off. "But you do have those wandering eyes," she muses, tongue making a soft tsking sound. "We will have to work on those."

Steve stares at her, now fully focused on her face again, though his mouth has gone dry. "You..."

"Mistress," she corrects him. "When you speak to me, you will call me Mistress."

"Yes, Mistress," Steve says, and his belly tightens along with his cock at the words.

Katharine nods, pleased. "Good," she tells him. "Now go inside, sit down on the kitchen chair, and take off your shoes."

As he turns to obey, Steve wonders at the specificity of her instructions. How long since someone told him exactly what to do like that? He must have still been a child.

The hallway ends in a large open room. A black couch lines the wall to his right, across from the small entertainment center. Between them is a large picture window with a view of the skyline that puts everything else in the apartment to shame. There are sheer white curtains, but they have been pushed to one side to reveal the cityscape outside. Directly before him is an entrance to a galley kitchen, and to the right is a small dinette with four chairs. The chair closest to him has been pulled out from the table and turned around. Steve assumes this is for him and he sits obediently, taking in the door to a small terrace between the table and the TV. He wonders if the outside patio wraps around the kitchen, remembers the doorman and the state of the lobby in this building, and decides that it must. He hopes that they will go outside at some point. The fall weather has definitely arrived with a chill, but not enough to make him shiver. The night air would be even more delicious with naughtiness.

Steve bends down to remove his shoes, glad that he didn't decide to tuck in his shirt because there is the slight chance that it may ride up in the back and reveal the bright pink lace panties he is wearing beneath his pants.

He wants those to be a surprise.

Steve pauses at his socks, wondering if he should take them off as well. She hadn't said to. He places his shoes underneath the chair and sits back, ready for her next command.

Katharine stands at the end of the entry hallway, eyes taking in the sight before her. "I think," she begins in a low voice, "that you are wearing far too many clothes."

Steve looks down at his shirt and pants, then back up at her. He waits, resisting the urge to pull off his shirt immediately.

Katharine nods her approval at his patience. "Good. Now, the shirt first, I think. Put it on the table behind you."

Steve tugs the shirt over his head in one swift move, then turns to deposit it as instructed. As he turns back around, Katharine has taken the few steps across the room toward him. She reaches a lazy finger out to touch his white tank top, plucking the shoulder strap between two fingers. She is so close he can smell her, her hair a hint of lavender, her skin a musk of vanilla, and he resists the urge to close his eyes and breathe her in.

"I haven't seen one of these since I lived at home with my father," she comments. "So old school." She takes a step to place herself squarely between his knees, placing both hands hard on his shoulders. "Too bad for you I don't have daddy issues," she says, fingers stroking quickly down his chest to tug the undershirt up and over his head. He feels it go with a slither of cotton against his skin, the feeling replaced by her hair as she quickly straddles him over the top of the chair. He can hear the stockings rubbing against his pants and wishes she would take those off so he can feel it against his skin. His hands reach out to caress her, to stroke those legs and that ass as she perches atop his hips.

"Oh no," she tells him in a decisive voice. "No touching for you. Not yet." She reaches behind him to retrieve something on the table behind him. "In fact," she says, "no looking either." He feels the blindfold as it hooks behind his ears and covers his surprised eyes, and then Steve sinks into a world of pure sensation. Katharine is still sitting on his lap, but he keeps his hands carefully at his sides, wanting to touch her but loving the feeling in his stomach that grows each second that he cannot.

She runs her hands down his face and around his neck, soft lips tracing fire around his collarbone as her hair brushes his nipples and causes the hair on his arms to stand erect.

His pants are incredibly tight, and he shifts his weight to relieve some of the pressure. "That must be so uncomfortable for you," she whispers against his skin, rubbing herself against his throbbing erection ever so slightly. Her hands trace light lines up his side, and he shivers, unable to stop himself from moving. He is smiling, a wide grin, and as her hands graze his skin, he giggles a little, the sensation a little too close to tickling.

Her hands stop at the sound, pressing hard and flat against his skin. "Oh no," she orders. "No sounds from you now. And certainly not any giggling." To punctuate her point, she arcs her fingers into little pinchers, tracing along his skin, pressing hard and then soft at intervals. Steve's face is turning red at the effort of restraint, his hands flexing uncontrollably at his sides.

"If you control it," she tells him, her breath warm on his skin, "you will be rewarded."

Her fingers skim down to the waist of his pants, pressing along the band and then sliding inside. He waits for the pause when she discovers the silky panties he wears, but if she is surprised, she doesn't show it with her hands.

"Naughty boy," she whispers, and her fingers begin their teasing again. He tenses, body straining against her touch, wanting to laugh and trying desperately to keep it in, his cock hard against the satin confines of the panties. He moves a little on the seat, wanting to use his hands to adjust, but unwilling to disobey her order.

"Well done," she tells him when he restrains the urge to giggle once more. Her fingers work deftly at his waist, and then his pants are open. "Off," she says, standing up as she helps him move just enough to slip the pants off his hips. The khaki makes a lovely sound as it slides past the silky panties, and he represses another shiver. He knows it's not the forbidden giggle, but he wants to do all that she asks of him.

The pants slide down his legs, and then her hands are pulling them off, and he feels her kneel before him, her body warm against the inside of his legs. Her hands run teasing lines up and down his thighs, then inside his legs, and then up to where his cock waits, uncomfortably hard and tucked inside the restrictive panties.

"Oh, my," she says in a low voice. "You do have an issue there." Her hands move slowly, oh so slowly up the expanse of the panties, resting on the thin fabric that his shaft presses against. "Let's see," she comments, fingers moving delicately across the fabric, slipping it down with delicious slowness to release his throbbing erection. She doesn't remove the panties all the way, just pushes them down enough to let his cock free. The elastic band still presses hard against the base of his shaft, a reminder that he is not free, that she is in charge here. "Now," she says, and her tone is stern, "You will not make a sound. Understood?"

"Yes, Mistress."

Warmth engulfs his shaft, and he almost loses it right there, letting out a moan as he comes from the sensation. But somehow, he manages to hold on. She slides his cock in and out of her mouth slowly, delicately, not in any rhythm regular enough to bring him to the edge, and he's sure he will be able to do this, to please her, but then her hands start sliding up his side, fingers teasing and tickling, and the conflicting sensations are too much—the warm demands of her mouth and the deft pressure of her hands on his sensitive skin combining to test his limits, and he shudders, a giggle bursting free as he pulls away from her, a move he tries to control but cannot.

She retreats slowly but deliberately from his cock, tongue and lips leaving emptiness behind, and he pushes his hips up, trying to follow the sensation, but he can feel her pulling away, hands leaving his side as she stands up. He feels her leaning in before she speaks, her voice low and disappointed.

"Naughty boy," she tells him, and not in the sexy way she had commended his panties. "You didn't listen." At this, she lets out a sigh, and then her hands are sliding up his sides again, not tickling as before, but business-like and efficient. She reaches his shoulders, and then both hands slide up and pluck the blindfold from his eyes. "No coming for you today," she tells him, placing the blindfold on the table and taking a step away.

"Mistress, may I speak?" he begins, then waits for her to give permission.

"Go on," she says, face curious.

"I am sorry that I did not please you today. How can I make it up to you?"

She considers, cocking her head to the side as she stares at him. "Very well." She steps closer again, leaning forward so that her breasts are right in front of his face. Her hands reach down and pull the panties back up over his cock. "We will call this the One Week Challenge."

"And what is the challenge?" he asks. Katharine reaches behind him to grab his pants from the table, then hands them to him. As he stands and starts to put them on, she continues, "I want to see you again one week from tonight. Until then, you are not allowed to touch yourself."

Steve pauses with his hands on his zipper. "Define touching myself."

She steps forward again, her hand reaching out to cup his still hard cock. "This," she says, squeezing a little to emphasize what she means, "is mine. You may touch it as needed for the necessary parts of life, but you are not allowed to touch yourself for pleasure until I see you again."

"So no coming at all?"

"Absolutely no coming," she reiterates. "No touching that isn't required at all. This," she squeezes again, harder this time, and Steve's stomach does another one of those odd little excited flops, "is mine."

Steve nods, and she releases him.

"If you succeed, you will be rewarded," she grins, "but if you fail, there will be consequences," and the sweet grin turns wicked in a way that makes his heart pound in anticipation. It's almost enough to make him want to fail.

Almost.

Chapter Three

The first day is easy, and Steve wonders if this challenge will be as simple as it seems. But in bed that night, his phone pings. Steve doesn't have many friends, and certainly no one who would send him a message late at night. He picks it up and swipes the screen, cock already stiffening at the image of her face.

[KATHARINE: And how is my Naughty Boy doing so far?]

[STEVE: Very well, Mistress.]

Steve pauses, then bites his lip and types more.

[STEVE: Maybe this challenge is too easy, Mistress.]

There is a pause, and the phone buzzes again. This time there is no text, only a close-up of Katharine's tits, round and glorious with perky nipples. There is nothing identifiable in the picture, no hint of face or other body parts—just those amazing breasts in his face.

Steve's cock hardens immediately at the sight. A moment later, the phone buzzes again.

[KATHARINE: Still too easy for you?]

The picture of the breasts is still visible above her words, and Steve gets greedy.

[STEVE: Maybe a little bit, Mistress.]

He grins, a small thrill in his belly as he waits for her reply. He is not disappointed. A minute later, the phone buzzes again. This time, a hand is wrapped around one breast, fingers tipped with red nail polish squeezing the hard nipple. Steve's cock jerks a little in his pants, and his hand slides down to touch himself. The phone buzzes before he can reach himself.

[KATHARINE: Remember the rules. No touching. That cock is MINE.]

Steve's hand drifts away from his hard cock, a slow ache growing in his balls. Maybe this week wouldn't be as easy as he thought.

Three days later, Steve is squirming on his bed, hands trapped beneath the small of his back, willing himself not to touch his hard dick. Katharine had sent two more pictures that night—one of her long leg encased in a black stocking, the other a close-up of her lips painted with fuck-me-red lipstick.

Five days later, Steve stands in the cold shower, trying not to see the words Katharine had sent that day.

You can do this, he tells himself, cock standing hard at attention despite the temperature of the water.

[KATHARINE: Imagine my mouth sucking on MY cock when I see you again. My tongue flicking the tip before I take it all the way inside to the back of my throat.]

That had almost undone him, but the next message sent him straight into the shower.

[KATHARINE: Imagine this silky pussy clenching around MY cock as I ride my way to pleasure. If you're lucky, I may bend you over before the end and have my way with that sweet asshole as well. I bet no one else has ever touched you there, not the way you want them to. Imagine how I will fuck that sweet ass until you beg for more.]

Standing in the shower, Steve lets the water run off his head and drip onto his hard cock. The image of her fucking him has him more excited than he expected. Of course, he's always excited by the thought of a girl riding his cock, but Katharine promising to peg him touches on desires he has barely begun to admit to himself.

I wonder what it will feel like, he muses, one hand trailing down first his hip and then sliding around to cup the round edge of his ass. Reaching just a little more, his finger brushes the edge of his asshole, and he shivers. His cock jerks. Steve takes his other hand and reaches down between his legs, avoiding his cock, but gripping his balls, sliding down just a little more to that sweet spot right between. Pleasure arcs through him.

I'm not touching my cock, he tells himself. *This is fine.*

Her cock, he reminds himself, both fingers pressing harder now. He imagines her lips, lipstick red like in the picture she sent, wrapping around his cock.

Still. Not. Touching. My...

The fantasy Katharine in his mind reaches out and tickles him mercilessly, never losing the rhythm of her mouth on his cock, and pleasure explodes over him. Cum sprays out into the shower, and Steve yanks his hands up, eyes widening.

Fuck.

Chapter Four

A week later, Steve stands in the hallway of Katharine's building, waiting until exactly 9pm to knock on her door. He bites his lip nervously, knowing that he will have to confess his crimes tonight. Excitement builds in his belly as he imagines the punishment she may inflict.

Maybe she'll beat me, he thinks, a small burn of hope in his chest. *Maybe she'll tease me again.*

He pictures those delicious lips around his cock again, the warm heat of her making his cock stir to life despite himself. He tries to think of anything else, to calm down, but nothing helps. Any thought of Katharine only excites him more.

So when his watch shows 9:00, he knocks on her door with a raging hard-on. The door opens immediately, Katharine stepping aside to let him inside.

She wears a sexy teddy in green, the satin and lace complementing her skin and hair, though Steve can't stop staring at her tits plump and teasing him above the top of the low cups. She is barefoot this time, no stockings, and her hair is down, flowing over her shoulders and down her back.

"Take off your shoes," she orders, though her voice is softer than it can be, a strong suggestion rather than a command. Steve bends down to remove his shoes, abandoning them near the front door. "Take a seat," she tells him, gesturing to the same kitchen chair as last time. Steve obeys, quickly adjusting his cock through his pants as he sits.

Katharine walks slowly over to stand before him, her red toenails a perfect contrast against the hardwood floor. "So," she says, "how is my cock this evening?" She kneels before him, reaching up to stroke him through his pants. "Eager to get to it, I see." Unbuckling his belt, she bites her lip as she quickly undoes the button and lowers the zipper.

Steve waits for her response to his white lace panties, and he is rewarded with a big grin as she slides his pants down and off. "Nicely done," she praises him. "A good choice." She sits back on her haunches, those perfect breasts on display even with his lap. His cock strains against the lace.

"Now," she says, "how was my cock this week?"

Steve gulps, biting his lip as he looks down at her, knowing her tone will shift with his next words.

"Well..." he stalls.

Katharine leans back, face intense as she stares up at him. "Well what?" When he doesn't respond, Katharine sits up on her knees and slides his cock free of the panties. Her grip is hard, bordering on unpleasant. "What did you do with my cock this week, Naughty Boy?"

At her words, his cock hardens even more, and she narrows her eyes at him, hand scooting down to cradle his balls. "I thought we had an understanding," she tells him, gripping harder, pleasure spilling over into pain, but a small burst of joy explodes deep in his gut, and he holds back a smile.

"I am sorry, Mistress," he says.

Her hand tightens a little bit more, a burst of pain followed by that sweet joy. "Why are you sorry, Naughty Boy? What have you done with my cock?"

"I didn't touch it, Mistress!" he bursts, unable to stop himself. His cock jerks involuntarily in her grip, and she loosens a little bit.

"I believe you," she says, coaxing now. "So what did you touch?"

"Other parts," he whispers.

"Tell me," she demands. "Where did you touch yourself?"

Steve looks away from her demanding eyes, staring at the floor. "My ass," he admits, "and my balls."

"I see," Katharine purrs. "And what happened when you touched yourself?"

"I came," he confesses, gaze swinging back to meet hers, wanting to see her reaction.

"Do you remember the rules we established last week, Naughty Boy?" she asks, hand perfectly still on his cock. Steve longs for her to move against him, even if it is to squeeze him again. Any kind of sensation will do.

He nods. "I wasn't supposed to come," he says. "I wasn't supposed to touch myself."

Katharine smiles. "And you broke the rules," she tells him. "Now, what do you suppose should happen to naughty boys who break the rules?"

"They get beaten?" Steve asks, unable to stop the hopeful note that creeps into his voice. The image of her hands on his skin, or another implement smacking him, is arousing. The idea of being completely at her mercy is intoxicating.

Katharine smirks, no doubt knowing what he wants from her. "Maybe," she says, "but only obedient boys get beaten properly. Naughty boys need to be taught a lesson, so that the next time, they follow the rules."

"Yes, Mistress." Steve looks down at the floor, waiting for her punishment.

Katharine ponders for a moment, then releases his cock, sliding his panties up with business-like efficiency. "Stand up," she commands, getting to her feet. Steve obeys. "Take off your shirt," she tells him. Steve tugs his shirt and undershirt over his head, then stands there in his little white panties, cock straining against the delicate lace, waiting for her next command. "Follow me," she orders, then heads deeper into the apartment, down a short hallway, and into a bedroom in the back corner.

A king-sized bed with a headboard perfect for bondage occupies most of the room, but instead of leading him to that, Katharine walks across the room to a dresser. She bends down, giving him a glorious view of her perfect ass in the g-string of the teddy, opens the bottom drawer, and pulls something out. Standing back up, she turns around, letting him see the device she holds. It is a metal contraption about the size of her palm with thick metal wires forged into a familiar shape.

"Do you know what this is?" she asks.

Steve nods. He's never seen a cock cage in person before, but he has the internet, and he's done his fair share of searches trying to scratch the itch deep inside. "Yes, Mistress."

"Have you used one before?" she continues.

Steve shakes his head. He's never been brave enough to try one before.

Katharine nods. "Good. This is perfect, then." She takes a few steps toward him, holding the device on the palm of her hand so he can see it more closely. "This part goes over your balls," she explains, finger circling the larger ring at the back, "and this is for my cock," she continues, running a finger along the curved cylinder of concentric circles. She flicks the small padlock on the front, twisting the key and opening the cage. "This key is mine, just like this cock is mine." She reaches out, sliding the panties down just enough to reveal his straining cock.

She sighs, shaking her head. "This will not do." She frowns, contemplating, then nods, struck by an idea. She hands him the cock cage along with the padlock and key. "Wait here."

She leaves him alone in the bedroom, and Steve examines the device. It will be restrictive, but it won't interfere with his ability to pee. He is glad that this cage doesn't include a sounding tip like some of the ones he has seen online. Maybe someday he will be ready to stick things inside his penis, but he's just not there yet.

He knows that he can't have a raging hard-on and put the cage on, and once on, it will make any erection he gets uncomfortable, bordering on painful, but the thought of wearing the cage and not having any way to remove it is exciting.

He will be at her complete mercy.

A shiver runs through him at the idea, and his cock jerks again. Steve hears Katharine's footsteps in the hallway behind him, but he doesn't turn to see her enter the room, staying exactly where he was as instructed.

When she reaches around him from behind, rubbing her breasts against his bare back, he is pleasantly surprised.

When she grabs his cock and cups his balls with a handful of ice, the shock goes through his entire body like an electric current. He stiffens, drops the cock cage, and then hunches over as the pain explodes through him. Katharine does not let go, moving with him as he huddles over himself, her grip merciless as the ice burns his sensitive skin.

Several agonizing moments pass before she releases him, and Steve sinks the rest of the way to the floor, kneeling first and then sliding onto his side, breath coming in shaking gasps. Katharine pushes on his hip, rolling him so he lays on his back on the cold floor, melted ice water dripping down between his ass cheeks to puddle on the floor beneath him. Most of the ice has melted, but her hands are still frigid when she grips him again, fitting the seemingly warm cock cage over his now limp penis. She grins wickedly as she snaps the padlock shut, then removes the key and slides it down the front of her teddy to nuzzle against her perfect breasts.

"Now," Katharine says, "perhaps this time you will follow the rules." She offers a hand to help Steve to his feet, and she leads him from the bedroom, down the hall, and back to where his pants and shirt still lay where he discarded them. She helps him dress, gentle but not inviting, even bending down to help with his shoes.

"So," she says when he is fully dressed and standing before her, "will you be a good boy this time for me?"

Steve nods, body still recovering from the shock. "Yes, Mistress," he manages, his voice unsteady.

"I have a long weekend coming up," Katharine says. "I expect you here on Friday night at 9pm, prepared to spend all three days with me."

"Yes, Mistress," Steve agrees.

"Until then, I will keep this key to my cock," she tells him. "There will be no playing with yourself—and there will be absolutely no coming until I allow it."

"Yes, Mistress," Steve says, that small burn in his belly back again at the idea of the next 48 hours spent at her mercy.

He can hardly wait.

Chapter Five

Two nights later, Steve paces in the hallway outside of Katharine's door. He adjusts himself, glad that despite the discomfort of the last two days, he still managed to wear a pair of green silky panties.

He hasn't touched himself except for the bare minimum, and while the idea of the cock cage is exciting, and knowing that he cannot free himself is thrilling, two days is a very long time to be restrained, and Steve is ready for his punishment to be over.

He knocks at precisely the hour as instructed, and Katharine lets him in immediately. Steve only takes a brief moment to appreciate her outfit, the dark blue satin robe hugging her curves and ending at the apex of her thighs. She leads him to the familiar kitchen chair and directs him to sit.

"And how is my Naughty Boy tonight?" she purrs. "Have you learned your lesson?"

"Oh yes, Mistress," Steve says, squirming on the chair. He hasn't been able to sit for very long, his sensitive skin nearly raw in some places from the metal rings. It hasn't been too painful beyond the morning wood he couldn't avoid, but the morning's erection lasted longer than he wanted, encouraged by thoughts of Katharine, and the metal rings dug in certain places. Luckily, his job allows him to work from home, and he can do most of what he needs at his convertible standing desk. He never thought he'd need to elevate the desk because of a cock cage, but he's not sorry for the experience.

Though he is ready for it to be over.

Katharine leans down, hands reaching for his belt and slowly, gently unbuttoning his pants. "Let's see my poor battered cock," she coos. "I'm so proud of you!" she exclaims at the sight of his green panties. "These are lovely!"

Steve smiles, that low thrill back in his belly at the idea of pleasing her. "Thank you, Mistress," he says quietly.

"Oh you poor thing," she says, sliding down the panties to reveal his cock jammed against the rings of the cage. She meets his eyes. "Will you follow the rules in the future?" she asks, a command in the words.

Steve nods. "Oh yes, Mistress. What do you want me to do?"

Katharine purses her lips, contemplating. Finally, she nods, then reaches into a small pocket in her robe and retrieves the key. A quick flick of her fingers, and the cage is removed, his cock free, and Steve sighs at the new ache that spreads from his balls. "There you go," she says, setting the cage on the table behind him. She sits back on her haunches, then stands up, holding out a hand to help him stand.

Steve obeys, the bottom of his shirt brushing against his tender cock, and a shiver runs through him. Katharine reaches out and slides both shirts over his head, pressing her breasts against his chest as she does so, the motion of his shirt replaced by the satiny feel of her robe against his skin. Steve takes a deep breath, trying to calm himself, not wanting to disappoint her again.

"Come with me," she says, then takes his hand and leads him down the hallway to the back bedroom. Instead of making him stand in the middle of the floor like last time, though, she leads him through another door into a master bathroom. She lets go of his hand when she walks over to the huge walk-in shower, opening the glass door and leaning in to turn on the water. Her robe scoots up a little, revealing the glorious bottom of her ass cheeks, and Steve hardens a little bit, the feeling quickly followed by another ache.

Standing up, Katharine smiles at him, then reaches for the tie at her waist. She removes it, then lets the robe fall open, revealing a body that Steve has only fantasized about. Perfect breasts, a flat stomach, a waxed pussy, and those long luscious legs. She lets the robe slide down her shoulders slowly, abandoning it when it falls to the floor around her feet.

"Come in," she says, reaching out her hand to him again. "Let me see to my obedient boy."

Steve takes her head and lets her lead him into the shower. The water is warm, pulsing from several rainshower jets in the ceiling, the kind of shower Steve has only seen in porn. There is a small bench at the back of the large space, but the shower stall is big enough for him to lie down easily. Katharine pulls Steve to the center of the shower, then begins to lather him in soap and scrub him gently with a loofah sponge. The water stings his raw skin at first, but then Steve forgets about it as other sensations overwhelm his senses: Katharine's warm, wet skin sliding across his as she washes his back, her fingernails against his scalp as she washes his hair, the gentle press of her hands as she washes his cock and balls.

"Don't come," she orders. She rinses him, then takes him gently in her mouth, the feeling of her warmth only slightly cooler than the hot water. She sucks him slowly, easily, teasing his length as she kneels before him, eyes closed as the water runs down her body.

Steve tries to calm down, to think of other things, but it's too much, and he grabs her head, pulling himself out of her mouth just before he comes. "I—" he manages, gasping. "I can't—" He looks down at her disappointed face. "Mistress, I..."

Katharine sighs, getting to her feet. "And here I thought you understood the rules."

"I do, Mistress. You're just so good at that. I can't help myself."

"Good at what, Naughty Boy?" she asks, standing up and pressing a hand to the center of his chest.

"Good at sucking cock, Mistress," Steve replies, stepping slowly as she continues to press him back. "You are so beautiful," he whispers to the goddess pushing him to the bench.

"Sit," she commands, and he obeys, sitting on the edge of the bench, his face even with her breasts. She frowns, no doubt thinking of what to do with him, then she smiles at him. "You think I'm beautiful, Naughty Boy?"

Steve nods. "Oh yes, Mistress. So fucking perfect. My goddess."

Katharine raises an eyebrow. "Goddess?" she echoes. "Then show me how you worship your goddess, Steve."

"May I touch you, Mistress?"

Katharine nods.

"Fuck yes," Steve moans, leaning forward to suck her nipple, using one hand to fondle the other one while his other hand slides down the curve of her waist to cup her hip. He sucks hard, then nibbles gently, looking up to see her reaction.

Katharine smiles, pleased. Steve grins, moving his mouth to her other nipple as he slides both hands down to rest on her hips. He releases her nipple to look down at the smooth skin of her pussy. He slides off the bench to his knees, hands drifting down to caress her thighs. He looks up at her, water running down his face, but he blinks through it. "May I lick your pussy, Mistress?" he asks, fingers hovering just outside the perfect spot between her legs.

Katharine nods, a wry grin crossing her lips. "You may try. But naughty boys often don't know how to do a proper job of it," she tells him.

"I will try," Steve agrees, then leans in, using his hands to separate her legs a little bit so he has room to work. Steve may not be a perfect lover, but there are certain skills he excels at, and licking pussy is one of them, drilled into him by his first lover, a woman who demanded several oral orgasms before she would even think about letting him put his cock inside of her. Steve didn't mind. He enjoys the sounds that women make when he finds the perfect spot, the exact rhythm.

Steve moves slowly, licking her skin in lazy strokes while he eases his fingers lower to run the outside of her opening. Katharine stiffens, and when Steve looks up, he sees that she is watching him carefully, eyes calculating. He rubs the outside of her opening again, sliding his thumbs gently against the sensitive skin, and her legs tighten—a good sign. Steve leans forward, mouth going to work immediately, licking her clit with careful strokes, noting when her legs stiffen and when she relaxes. When he figures out the spots she prefers and the rhythm she wants, he wraps one arm around her, cupping her ass and holding her close. His other hand continues to rub slowly, fingers slipping in and out of her in matching rhythm to his tongue.

Katharine moans, her hands reaching down to twist in his hair, and Steve continues to lick in the same rhythm, knowing that she is close now. He adds another finger inside her, and she tightens immediately, hips shuddering as he continues to lick her clit.

"Oh fuck!" she cries, hands latching onto his head as her body shakes in his arms. Steve tightens the arms around her back, supporting her weight as her legs turn rubbery, continuing to nuzzle her clit until she tells him to stop. "That was well done," she says when she catches her breath, looking down at him between her legs. "Exceptionally well done," she admits.

"May I lick your pussy some more, Mistress?" Steve asks. "It's so delicious. I just want to lick you all night long."

Katharine preens, enjoying his words, but she shakes her head. "I don't think I can stand for another orgasm like that," she admits. "My legs are Jell-O."

"Then sit on my face," Steve suggests, swiveling his body so he sits on his butt, then scooting down so he lays on his back on the floor between her legs. "Let me eat that pussy some more, Mistress," he begs. "I need you on my face."

"I'll be the one needing things," she orders, but she kneels over him, moving up so her legs are on either side of his face. Slowly, she lowers herself until her body touches his lips. Steve gives her a moment to get situated, her hands resting on the bench behind him, then reaches both hands up to grip her ass. This is his favorite position. He grips her tightly, refusing to let her move, then attacks her clit again, the same steady strokes he now knows she likes while one hand slips below his chin and into her again, pressing up and forward to stroke her g-spot. Katharine moans, hips rocking, but his arm holds her steady. He breathes through his nose, loving the spectacle above him, Katharine's perfect breasts jutting out, her hair a riot of darkness and water as she tilts her head back and forth in her pleasure.

"Fucking yes!" she yells, and then she is shuddering again, thighs thrumming against his face as the orgasm rips through her. "You are quite talented for a Naughty Boy!"

"Again, Mistress?" he begs, but Katharine is already pulling away, sliding down to sit on his chest before she leans forward and kisses him hard, tongue eager in his mouth, tracing the line of his teeth.

"I'm going to fuck you, Naughty Boy," she tells him, sucking on his lips. "You deserve it after that performance."

"Thank you Mistress," Steve says, watching as she slides that glorious body farther down, settling herself above the hard rod of his cock.

"You are not allowed to come," she orders, then slams down with a jerk of her hips, engulfing him completely.

Steve's eyes close as the intensity of her pussy around his cock overwhelms him, and then open again. He wants to watch her ride him, wants to see those perfect titties bounce and jerk as she moves faster.

"That's good," she groans, leaning back as she lifts herself up and then back down on him, pressing him deep inside. "That's so fucking good!"

"Can I touch you, Mistress?" Steve asks, hands fisted at his side as he longs to caress those tits.

"You may," she allows, moving again.

Instead of reaching to cup her breasts as he desires, Steve moves his hands to press against her clit again, using one to grip her round ass as the other rubs a small circle over her clit. Katharine looks down at his hand and then his face, a wide smile on her face. "You are good!" she exclaims. Steve continues to rub, watching her breasts but also focusing on his hands because he knows if he spends too much time watching her tits bounce in front of his face, he's going to lose it and come. If he tries to grip them, it will all be over.

Instead, he concentrates on making Katharine come again, this time on his cock, and the grip of her pussy almost sends him over the edge, but he manages to pull back at the last moment, both hands on her hips holding her steady under the guise of supporting her after her orgasm.

Katharine catches her breath, then leans down to kiss him again, the water rushing over them both. "Very nice," she tells him. "I may even let you lick my pussy again."

"Thank you, Mistress," Steve says, looking up at the gorgeous woman still atop him.

It's going to be a long weekend, and he's looking forward to every moment.

Chapter Six

Steve stands in the center of Katharine's bedroom, staring at himself in the full-length mirror on her closet door. He wears a classic French maid outfit: black dress with a white apron, black ribbon tied around his neck, white thigh high stockings connected to black garters, and a pair of sensible low heels that he can actually walk around in.

Steve doesn't ask how Katharine has the outfit in his size, especially the shoes. He wants to assume she ordered it for him; she spent enough time undressing him over the last few weeks, enough time for her to see his sizes and order it. Though the idea that she has other men in her house, completing the same tasks, is both intimidating and exciting.

He is officially Katharine's Naughty Boy now.

Steve adjusts the small white cap on his head, smirking at his reflection. He's never thought about fully crossdressing before, but he finds he enjoys the experience, especially the padded bra wrapped over his shoulders and clipped behind his back. It took a few tries to figure out the motion, but Katharine helped him. Looking at his reflection, Steve decides that when this is over, he might order some more clothing of his own and explore his options.

But for now, he's going to enjoy every moment of this weekend.

Nodding at himself, he heads into the living room, finding Katharine resting on the couch, feet propped beneath her as she leans on the arm of the couch, book open on her lap.

"Mistress?" he asks quietly.

"You can start in the kitchen," she says, gesturing to the galley kitchen behind him.

Steve nods, then heads into the kitchen, enjoying the tap of the heels as they echo on the wooden floor. He wipes down the counters first, tidying items and putting everything in the cabinets where he finds similar items. The dishes are easy enough: a single plate, silverware, a glass cup, and one small pan.

While he works his way through her refrigerator, cleaning the shelves and organizing her food, he heats up a pot of water on the stove, delivering his mistress a hot cup of tea, along with several tea cookies, on a small tray. She smiles her approval at the gesture, then nods to the small door in the hallway. Steve opens it to find a broom and mop snapped into a rack on the inside of the door, a bucket on the floor, and shelves of messily jammed towels and sheets.

Steve rolls his shoulders, gearing up for his next task, then empties the entire contents of the closet onto the kitchen table. He folds the towels into the exact same size, piling them according to color, then fights the sheets and blankets into similar submission, tidying her closet with the same efficiency that he used in her kitchen. Seeing the finished product excites him a little, but not as much as her nod of approval at the sight.

He continues his cleaning, sweeping her entire house and then mopping the kitchen and living room, gently lifting her feet back onto the couch when he moves beneath her. While the floor dries, he moves into the bathroom, scrubbing the shower and tub until they shine. He doesn't know Katharine has appeared behind him until something smacks his bare ass while he is on his knees cleaning the toilet. His body jerks, cock hardening instantly at the impact, and he pauses, eagerly waiting for the next blow.

It doesn't come.

After a long moment, Steve looks over his shoulder to see Katharine standing behind him holding a small plastic ruler. She nods at the toilet, and Steve turns back to his work.

A moment later, another smack lands across his ass, and he jerks forward, cock pressing against the cold porcelain for a brief second before he pulls back—right into another smack. Steve redoubles his efforts, wanting to finish cleaning and stand up before he loses control and comes all over the clean floor. Katharine watches him work, but she doesn't smack him again.

When he finishes the bathroom, she leads him toward the bedroom, opening three dresser drawers to reveal a trove of sex toys. She hands him the spray cleaner and a roll of paper towels, then sets herself up on the bed, watching him as she lazily flips through a magazine. Steve grins, cock hard but not on the edge of exploding, then gets to work. He lays out each item on the top of the dresser, working through one drawer at a time. There is an array of dildos in different shapes and sizes: some that vibrate, some with wide suction cup bases, some of glass and metal. The prostate massagers are next, a series from small to obnoxiously large.

When Steve finishes those, Katharine gets off the bed and approaches him. "Kneel on the floor," she tells him, "and lay your chest on the bed." Her bed is low to the ground, so Steve obeys easily, his ass exposed as the maid outfit rides up his waist. The stockings tug against his thighs as the garters pull tight, a pressure he enjoys. He hears Katharine move over the dresser and then the sound of her picking something up off the top—an item he just cleaned then.

She approaches him from behind, sinking to her knees and sliding up to press her body against his skin. He enjoys the slide of her silk robe against his ass, but then her hands are sliding toward his cock, enfolding him gently and stroking ever so slowly. Her other hand finds his ass, and her fingers massage him, easing around the edge. Steve shudders at the combination of sensations, straining back against her, wanting more.

Her hands abandon him for a moment, and he hears the sound of a bottle being opened, then warm wet hands grasp his cock and rub his asshole at the same time. Katharine is gentle, careful to keep a slow rhythm on his cock with one hand as she presses her other thumb inside of him. When he eases, her thumb vanishes, replaced by something slightly larger, one of the prostate massagers he laid on top of the counter. Steve imagines the shape as it slowly fills his ass, small at first, then gradually larger until it reaches an apex and immediately shrinks again before the wide base. He tightens as the dildo presses deeper, and Katharine waits until he relaxes again, hand caressing his cock gently, pleasure building as he explores the new sensations. By the time she gets the entire dildo in his ass, Steve's cock is weeping, and Katharine is gentle as she tugs a stretchy rubber ring around his balls, securing the dildo in place.

"Stand up," she says quietly, backing away and letting Steve find his feet. The dildo in his ass is a new feeling, and he moves slowly, enjoying the pleasure as it hits different places inside of him. When he is back on his feet and fairly steady, Katharine smiles and gestures back to the dresser. "Continue," she says, leaving the room. Steve hears the water turn on the bathroom, presumably Katharine washing her hands.

He works his way through the rest of the drawers, unearthing a wide array of treasures: anal beads, leather whips, rubber flogs, a trove of buzzy bullets, and more restraints types than Steve imagined existed.

He hears Katharine re-enter the room just as he is finishing up. "Mistress, may I ask a question?"

Katharine nods. "Sure."

"Where did you get all of this stuff? The internet?"

Katharine smirks. "Fetish Circuit," she replies.

Steve cocks his head, nearly losing his little cap. He reaches up to straighten it. "What's that?" he asks.

"Continue to please me, Naughty Boy," Katharine purrs, "and I will show you."

"Thank you, Mistress," Steve says. "What next?" He is willing to do more work, but the dildo in his ass has him rock hard, and he will struggle not to come if she makes him do much more.

"I think you've paid enough attention to my home," she says, biting her lip. "I think it's time you paid some attention to me."

"Please, Mistress," Steve says. "What would you like? A massage? I can rub away all of your stress. Or your feet?" Steve glances at her bare feet. "Can I paint your toenails, Mistress? Rub your feet and suck your toes?"

Katharine laughs, then sits down on the bed with a shrug. "Sure. The nail polish is in the bathroom cabinet."

"What color?" Steve asks.

"Surprise me," Katharine replies, lying down so her robe reveals all of her gorgeous legs.

"Yes, Mistress," Steve replies, heading to the bathroom. He returns with more supplies than a bottle of nail polish, carrying a small tub filled with warm bubbly water and a towel, leaving once to collect a small bottle of massage oil.

Steve lifts her legs, gently placing her feet in the tub of water, removing one and rubbing it. He takes his time, sucking each toe as he promised. Katharine doesn't seem to enjoy it more than anything else, but Steve's cock weeps again as her delicate toes fill his mouth, loving the notion of literally licking his goddess's feet.

He is in the middle of sucking the toes on her other foot when she reaches a hand into the small pocket of her robe, and squeezes something inside. The dildo inside Steve's ass purrs to life, vibrations flooding through him.

Steve spits out her toe with a gasp, entire body electrified, and then Katharine squeezes again, and the sensation ceases, leaving

Steve shuddering. It is too much—he explodes into an orgasm, cum coating the inside of the maid's outfit.

"Did you just come, you Naughty Boy?" Katharine asks, removing her hand to show him a small black remote control.

"I'm sorry, Mistress," Steve gasps, still unable to say more.

Katharine frowns, then pushes the button again. The dildo vibrates again, this time stimulating incredibly sensitive flesh, and Steve hunches into himself, the pleasure too much to bear. Finally, Katharine stops. Steve spends a few moments catching his breath.

"I didn't know it would do that, Mistress," Steve says. "Please forgive me."

"Hmm," Katharine continues to frown. "You've been so good today. I wanted to reward you. Now you have to earn your way back into my graces." She gives him a stern look. "No more coming without permission," she orders. "Now I have to think about a punishment."

Steve nods, returning to her feet with double the attention as she ponders. When he paints her toenails, his execution is perfect, every line precise and not a single mark on her skin. He moves to her legs next, rubbing her with oil and easing the tension from her calves with strong hands. He pauses when she leans up.

"Move your leg over here," she demands. Steve leans back, swinging his lower body around so one stockinged leg rests on the bed next to her. She frowns at the low-heeled shoe on her blanket, and takes it off, chucking it aside to land on the floor. Her hands move quickly up his leg, efficient rather than sexy, seeking the hooks of the garter belt. She releases the top of the stocking, and it snaps down his leg, revealing a hairy thigh and large kneecap. Katharine nods, lifting a small group of hairs up and away from his skin with two fingers before releasing them to curl back against his thigh. "Take them off," she gestures at the stockings.

Steve stands up, fumbling with the hooks before letting the other stocking slide down. He is relieved to release the pressure around his thighs, but sorry to lose the silky feel of the stockings against his skin. He slides both down slowly, relishing the feel before tugging them off his feet.

"Now," she says, sitting up, "go to the bathroom, and bring back hot water in this tub, a towel, shaving cream, and the razor in the cabinet."

Steve's eyes widen as he realizes what she means to do. He has always fantasized about shaving a woman's legs, but he has never thought about shaving his own. He obeys, returning with the items. Katharine has him sit on the bed, then spreads the towel out beneath his legs.

A small grin crosses her lips as she looks up at his face. "Have you ever done this before?"

Steve shakes his head. "I've shaved my face," he says. "But that's it."

"So you should pay attention," Katharine suggests, and Steve nods.

She begins slowly, gently, dipping her hands in the warm water and running them over his legs to get them wet, then running a line of cream down one leg. She massages the cream, smearing the foam from his ankle to his thigh, and Steve pulls the dress out of the way to rest on his belly, exposing the crinoline. She takes the razor and makes a smooth line up his shin, the hair and shaving cream gathering on the razor to leave a mostly smooth swath of skin beneath. She rinses the razor in the water and repeats the motion, shaving his legs in delicate strips. She does an entire pass, then re-lathers him in foam and repeats the process, catching the stray hairs that still linger. Steve watches with a mix of erotic and clinical interest, learning the technique while soaking in the sensations.

When he has one smooth leg and one hairy leg, she hands him the razor. She lathers his leg, then guides his hand as he removes his hair, pressing harder here, and easier there. When he finishes, she gestures for him to stay where he is. She gathers the tub and heads into the bathroom; Steve hears the water running as she empties the dirty water. She returns with a small bottle of lotion, and slowly rubs down his legs, the cream soothing the irritated parts of his skin. Then, she takes his hand and runs it down the newly shaven skin. Steve shivers at the sensation, then looks at her.

"Mistress," he says meekly, hands on his thighs, "May I ask a question?"

"What is it?" Katharine replies, head cocked to one side as she considers their work.

"May I shave your legs?" he asks, the fantasy finally a possibility. "I would be so honored."

"Are you saying my legs are hairy?" she asks.

"Of course not, Mistress," he says, not wanting to upset her. He's not lying. She has the very beginning of stubble. He wouldn't have noticed if he didn't have a long-standing desire to shave a woman's legs.

Katharine sits back, pursing her lips. "You really want to shave my legs?"

"Please?" Steve asks, knowing there is a pleading note in his voice that he can't hide.

Katharine shrugs, flopping down on the bed. "Sure," she tells him with a shrug. "Let's see what you've learned."

"Oh, thank you, Mistress!" Steve practically leaps off the bed, returning a few minutes later with more supplies: a clean towel and a fresh tub of warm water.

"Are you ready, Mistress?"

Katharine is smiling, and she lets him watch as she reaches for the remote again, pressing the button and enjoying his expression as the vibrations tingle through him again. She turns it off after a moment, careful not to let him get too close again.

"I thought I should do that now, before you have a razor in your hand."

"Very wise, Mistress."

Steve doesn't speak as he works, spreading the shaving cream with soft strokes, rinsing the razor in the warm water after he runs it over the lines of her skin. He spends time rubbing the massage oil into her skin after he finishes, careful to moisturize those luscious legs.

His cock is hard again by the time he finishes and begins setting items aside. He puts everything away, then returns to find her still lying on the bed where he left her, face close to dozing.

"I think I may nap," she says. "That was so perfectly relaxing."

"Very well, Mistress," Steve says. "I will continue to clean."

Katharine nods, and Steve leaves her in the bed, returning to his tasks, enjoying the thrill of the dildo as he continues to please his mistress. The buzzing of the dildo tells him that she is awake again, and he returns to the bedroom to find her blinking lazily at him.

"You've been so good today. Mostly," she says. "You know what else a good maid does, my boy?" Katharine asks, sliding her robe up to reveal her smooth pussy.

"What's that, Mistress?" Steve asks, sitting down on the edge of the bed.

"He makes sure the mistress is completely satisfied in every way."

Steve nods, adjusting himself beneath the maid outfit, not wanting to embarrass himself again. "What would satisfy the Mistress?" he asks, moving closer.

Katharine's robe has slid up to puddle across her belly. As he watches, she tugs the sides apart, revealing those glorious breasts. Steve's cock hardens again, pressing awkwardly against the tulle underneath the maid's uniform. "I am here to serve," he breathes, shifting a little to move his cock away from the scratchy crinoline.

"Then I think you should lick this pussy, Steve," she orders, casually reaching over to the small pile of work material on the night table. She ignores the closed laptop, the file folders, instead plucking a familiar plastic ruler from the top of the pile and leaning up on her elbows. She gestures with the ruler. "I know how well you lick pussy, Steve. Let's see how well you can follow orders."

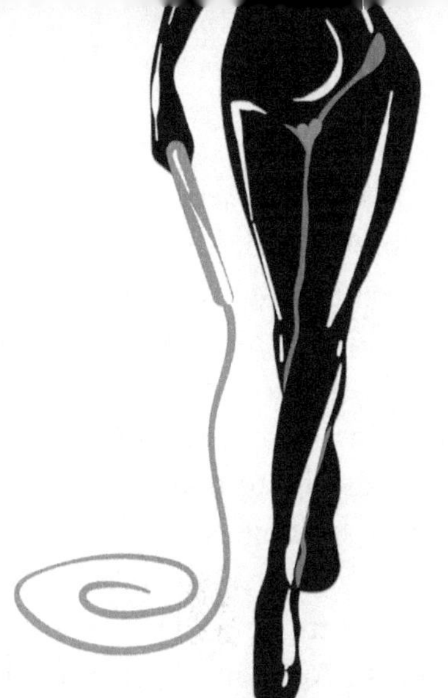

Chapter Seven

Steve tugs her closer to the edge of the bed, kneeling on the floor and settling himself between her thighs. He wants to be comfortable for a long while, but the dildo in his ass makes other positions too tantalizing, and he knows if he lays down, his cock rubbing against the bed as he moves will bring him too close to the edge.

He slides both hands under her thighs and moves her pussy closer, leaning down to breathe in her scent. He starts slowly, softly, with gentle kisses down her lips, fingers teasing her opening, allowing her to open to him, rocking her hips to give him better access.

"That's quite lovely," she moans, and Steve is rewarded by the joy of the dildo buzzing to life in his ass. He struggles to keep his current pace, fingers deftly circling the outer edge of her lips while his tongue moves ever closer to her clit. The dildo stops, and Steve is able to focus again.

"Suck my clit," she demands a moment later, and Steve obeys, nuzzling her clit with his tongue while sucking. "And finger me!" she adds. Steve's finger slides inside, marveling at her wetness, the way her pussy tightens on his fingers, imagining that his cock is inside her instead.

His dick jerks at the idea, and a few seconds later, the dildo vibrates again, his reward to following her instructions perfectly. Steve allows himself to enjoy the feeling, mouth working hard against her body, fingers sliding in and out, feeling her response and adjusting to her needs, and soon, her thighs tighten, pressing hard against his cheeks. Steve keeps the same rhythm, knowing that she needs him to focus in order to come. She shudders, pussy locking onto his fingers.

"Fuck yes!" she yells, a hand burying itself in his hair, knocking the white cap aside. "You are so good at that!" She gasps, then leans back. A second later, the vibration stops as she remembers the remote. "Sorry," she says. "I shouldn't have left that on so long."

"I am fine, Mistress," Steve says. "There's nowhere else I'd rather be than here, worshiping your pussy."

"Make me come again," she demands, whacking the top of his head with the ruler, "and I just may let you come tonight."

Steve bends his head down, mouth sucking her clit as his fingers slide back inside. He knows her body now, knows what she likes, and within minutes, she is on the edge again, the ruler thumping against his head as she urges him on.

"Oh, like that," she moans, "please keep doing that!" In her ecstasy, she has forgotten her role as Mistress, begging him for release. Steve chuckles, fingers moving in rhythm with his mouth, and then both her hands are wrapped in his hair, pressing him against her as her entire body shakes and shivers.

"Fuck yes!" she screams, shuddering against his face. Steve retreats, hands pulling out of her and cupping her ass as he rests his cheek on her thigh, waiting for her to regain her senses.

When Katharine's breathing regulates, she leans up to look down at him. "Naughty Boy," she says, "I think I may have to keep you."

"I'd like that, Mistress," Steve says, placing a kiss on her thigh.

"Will you follow the rules?" she asks.

"I will try," he says, knowing the hint of resistance will please her. She enjoys punishing him when he breaks the rules.

And he loves being punished.

"Very well," she says, sitting up all the way. She runs her hands through his hair, straightening the mess she made, then gently moves him off her thigh, standing up and walking over to the closet. Steve sinks to the side, sitting on the floor, the dildo pressing into him with delicious new friction.

Steve watches her walk, that glorious body flushed from orgasms and lovely as she opens the door. He's a bit curious to see the inside. Judging by the rest of her apartment, he expects a jumble of clothing. Instead, he is rewarded by a clean line of color-coded dresses next to perfectly sorted shirts and skirts. Two rows of shoes line the floor, from sandals to thigh-high boots folded over. She reaches for a small set of drawers in the center of the closet and removes an item. Steve sees that there are other similar items in the drawer, and he looks back at the perfectly organized clothes.

How many Naught Boys does she have? The idea that others have cleaned her house sparks both jealousy and joy. Steve doesn't want to be her one and only, doesn't want any of the normal relationship crap from her. He just wants to worship her, to please her, to be among those worthy enough to lick her pussy.

And the thought that another man, a stronger man, fucks her before he does starts a small fire in his belly that promises to devour him.

I want to watch, he decides. *At least once, I want to watch her with another man, and I want to lick the cum from her pussy.*

A slow smile crosses his face at the image, and when Katharine walks back over to him, she returns the smile. She holds a black leather collar in her hand, a thin band with a metal buckle and a silver loop that she can hook things to.

"Will you be collared by me?" she asks.

Steve nods, mouth suddenly dry. "Yes, Mistress."

"Come here then." She gestures to the floor in front of her.

Steve rocks onto his knees, crawling over to her. When he reaches her feet, he licks her toes, then sits back on his haunches. Katharine smiles, then unties the thin black ribbon tied around his neck. She drops it on the floor.

The leather is cool against his skin and tight when she buckles it. "You will wear this when you are with me," she tells him. "This shows me that you are my Naughty Boy."

"Yes, Mistress," Steve agrees, swallowing and feeling the restriction of the leather against his neck.

Katharine turns around, returning to the closet for one more item. Steve admires the curve of her ass as she turns.

She returns with another strip of leather, this one much smaller and more ordinary. She gestures for Steve's wrist and he lifts it up, letting her slide the leather bracelet around his wrist and tightening it against his skin. "You will wear this at all times. It's my mark on you," she says.

"Yes, Mistress," Steve says. "Thank you, Mistress."

"Now," she says, lifting him to his feet. Steve bobs on his feet for a second, readjusting to the low heels. The back of his feet will have blisters tomorrow, but he doesn't care.

"Yes, Mistress?" Steve asks, looking down at her from his full height, enhanced now by the shoes.

"Kiss me," she orders.

Steve bends down, meeting her lips with a soft kiss that quickly turns passionate. He has licked other parts of her body, had her mouth around his cock and her fingers in his ass, but he has never kissed her like this before, and the sensation is intoxicating. Their shower kisses were frantic but quick; this is long and filled with promise. His arms reach around her body, one hand cupping her ass and the other reaching around to squeeze one perfect titty. His cock jerks, hard against her belly, and her hands slide up his arms and around his neck, twisting in his hair as she explores his mouth.

"Undress," she whispers against his mouth. "I want to see you."

Steve lifts the dress over his head in one motion, eager to free his cock from the rough, and slightly crusty, crinoline beneath, then reaches around awkwardly to remove the bra. Katharine kneels before him as he steps out of the shoes, unhooking the garter and sliding each stocking down his legs. She leaves the dildo in place, hands carefully avoiding his cock as she undresses him. When he stands before her wearing only the collar, she stands up and grabs his hair in a fist.

"Now," she breathes against his mouth, gripping his hair painfully as she holds him in place, "I want you to fuck me, Naughty Boy. Fuck me hard. And well." She tugs on his head, looking at him intensely. "Fuck me well, Boy, and you will be allowed to come."

"Yes, Mistress," Steve says. He reaches out to cup her ass and lifts her. Katharine wraps her legs around his waist, taking some of the weight off his arms. Steve isn't a big guy, and he's not super strong, but Katharine is small, and he can carry her for a little while like this. The feel of her naked body rubbing against his is plenty of motivation to hold her tight.

Instead of taking her to the bed, as he imagines she expects him to, he walks over to the wall instead, resting her back against the wall exactly across the room from the full-length mirror he admired himself in earlier.

"Watch me fuck you, Mistress," he says, adjusting himself to line up his cock, then remembers he is her submissive. "Will you watch me fuck you?"

Katharine gasps, the idea delighting her as her gaze slips from his face to look over his shoulder, seeing herself pinned against the wall by his body. "Yes, Naughty Boy," she says. "Now fuck me well!"

Steve doesn't wait for more encouragement, pushing his cock inside of her in one hard thrust. Katharine moans, her pussy warm and soaking wet around his cock, and Steve pulls back and plunges in again. Katharine's eyes close as her head tilts back, completely lost in the sensation, and Steve reverts to his old bedroom habits, fucking her hard and fast, enjoying the thud of her back against the wall, the slapping wet sound of his body pounding into hers, the glassy eyed pleasure on her face.

The dildo in his ass intensifies every motion, but Steve holds himself back. He's on familiar territory here, and he knows how to wait to come, though the dildo adds another layer of pleasure to each stroke.

"How is that, Mistress?" he asks, but the words are more of a demand than a request, and then Katharine is shuddering on his cock, pussy gripping him hard as she comes. "You like coming on your cock?"

"So...good..." she moans, body going limp for a second.

Steve pauses, waiting for her to come back, cock buried deep inside of her. She has bitten his shoulder, the pain a dull thud only registering now that he has paused, but the mark will remain for several days. Steve wants more like them.

"May I continue, Mistress?" he asks, voice more submissive again.

"Please," she whispers. "I want more." Steve moves slowly at first, easing her back into the rhythm, and then she is gripping his shoulders hard, eyes skipping between the picture of them in the mirror behind him and the collar around his neck. When she is close again, she reaches up to grab his hair, looking deep into his eyes.

"Come for me, Naughty Boy," she orders. "I need you to come for me!"

Steve bends down, claiming her mouth with a painfully hard, bruising kiss, biting her lips and scorching her tongue as he pounds her against the wall, finally allowing himself to let go.

The orgasm screams through him, and Katharine yells out her release as they come together. He pumps a few more times, body still shuddering around the dildo, overwhelmed by the warm heat of her pussy, and then they both slowly slide down the wall to land in a crumpled heap on the floor. Steve ends up on his back on the floor,

Katharine's body wrapped around him. For a few long moments, neither speaks, each regaining breath and slowing pounding heartbeats.

Finally, Katharine sits up, the movement of her pussy pushing his cock out of her. She immediately reaches for it, adjusting her body so his soft dick presses against her again.

"Oh no," she groans, looking down at him, still breathing heavily on the floor. "That won't do." She reaches around, clearly searching for something on the floor.

The dildo in Steve's ass roars to life, and his cock jerks, hardening again as she finds the remote control.

"That's much better," she says, pushing his semi-erect cock back inside of her. "I expect my Naughty Boy to come at least two more times tonight."

Steve smiles up at her. "Yes, Mistress. As you wish."

Now You See Me

HONEY POT COLLECTION

Ali Whippe

Dedication

For all the boys who like to watch

Chapter One

12:01 pm [Dylan: Wake up, Sorina.]
12:03 pm [Sorina: Yes, Master. I am awake, sir. May I use the bathroom?]
12:04 pm [Dylan: You may. Finish your morning routine in eleven minutes. Text me when you are in the kitchen.]
12:04 pm [Sorina: Yes, Master.]
12:14pm [Sorina: I am in the kitchen, Master.]
12:14 pm [Dylan: You are early, Sorina. I may have to punish you later.]
12:15 pm [Sorina: As you wish, Master.]
12:16 pm [Dylan: You may have your coffee now, but no sugar today. Eat a strawberry yogurt.]
12:16 pm [Sorina: Thank you, Master. I will be more precise tomorrow.]
12:17 pm [Dylan: Yes, you will. I need you ready for tonight, though. Are you wearing the bra and panties I picked out?]
12:17 pm [Sorina: Of course, Master.]
12:20 pm [Dylan: Good girl. Send me pictures. Close-up of you wearing the bra first. Panties next. Then your entire midsection in one picture without knees or face.]
12:22 pm [Sorina: Download Attached Image.]

12:24 pm [Sorina: Download Attached Image.]
12:25 pm [Sorina: Download Attached image.]
12:30 pm [Dylan: Very nice, Sorina. You have done well. Now lay the dress you will wear tonight on the bed and send me a picture. Then a picture of your feet in the shoes I chose.]
12:33 pm [Sorina: Download Attached Image.]
12:34 pm [Sorina: Download Attached Image.]
12:37 pm [Dylan: Excellent. I will be there to pick you up at 10:00 tonight. I expect you to be ready.]
12:38 pm [Sorina: Yes, Master.]
12:39 pm [Sorina: Master, is there anything else I should do to prepare for tonight?]
12:40 pm [Dylan: Not yet. Get to work, Sorina. You have ten minutes before you need to leave. Remember the list.]

Sorina puts her phone down on the kitchen table and finishes the last sip of her coffee, putting the mug in the sink and tossing the empty yogurt container. Throwing on a pair of jeans and her Empire Records t-shirt, she checks herself in the mirror one more time before heading out for the day. Her simple makeup is enough to subtly flatter her normal good looks, highlighting her eyes and showcasing her pouty lips. She's glad she got the morning routine down to ten minutes—Dylan had been so disappointed when she still took over twenty minutes to get up. Now every motion is planned, each moment accounted for, and the general feeling of chaos doesn't take hold in her gut so easily. He'd been right, of course; simple routines help her so much. Him telling her what to wear helps more. His orders are always simple, direct, and within her ability—another thing that calms her raging nerves.

Her life is chaotic enough without having to make all those little decisions. Not that it's complicated—she works at a record store, finding vinyl albums for diehard fans who wander in but mostly packing up the orders that flow in online. She listens to music all day long, a perk, but sometimes the customers who do stroll in can be condescending. They see her long blonde hair and huge tits and assume she's just a pretty face. She doesn't bother telling them that she has their inventory memorized, that she can tell them where each album is in the store, nor does she mention that she plays six instruments and reads sheet music or that she can recite the history of most of the bands they carry—each album and track list burned into her brain.

Of course, all that knowledge makes it hard to recall other things, like the password for her bank account or where she put her keys. Dylan has helped with all that, establishing tiny routines and checking on her to make sure she follows through, punishing her when she fails.

Sorina likes the punishments a little too much sometimes, and occasionally she deliberately flouts an order just to see what will happen.

She obeys another of his commands before leaving, checking off each item on her mental list as he instructs: dinner—yes, phone—yes, purse—yes, keys—yes, everything turned off in the apartment—yes, lock the door—yes. She heads down the stairs, a bounce in her step as she walks the block to the store.

"Hey!" Jenelle says as Sorina walks through the glass door. The middle-aged owner of the record store sits at the long counter, a mostly eaten sandwich still open on the paper in front of her. "On time again!" Jenelle smiles, tucking dark hair behind her ear and pushing up her glasses as she looks Sorina over. "I don't know what you're doing, girl, but keep it up. It's working!"

Sorina smiles at her boss, thinking of Dylan's control in her life, and walks behind the counter to join her. She tucks the Tupperware containing her dinner in the small fridge behind the counter, checks to make sure the store keys are in her purse, then sets it in the drawer below the register. "I'm trying a new thing," Sorina says vaguely. "I like it."

"So do I!" Jenelle says, taking a final bite and crumbling the rest of the paper, tidying her lunch as she gets to her feet, abandoning the single stool behind the counter. She tosses everything in the trash can, then finishes the rest of her bottled water. Sorina has casually mentioned that Jenelle should just bring a bottle and keep refilling it, but her boss doesn't seem interested in conserving plastic. She's more into conserving vinyl albums. Sorina puts her large water bottle on the counter, a subtle gesture that is lost on her boss.

"I did all the orders from yesterday and this morning," Jenelle says, nodding at the clipboard next to the register—another wasteful habit of printing everything on paper—but Jenelle insists on her system. Sorina looks over at the table against the wall beyond the counter. A pile of packages rests there, waiting for the mail carrier to pick them up. A decent day, and it's early yet.

"Nice," Sorina says, settling onto the stool Jenelle abandoned. "Thanks." She looks around the small store, the racks of albums, the posters lining the available wall space. "Anything I should work on today?"

Jenelle shrugs. "Nah. You did a great job re-sorting the punk section last time. Take it easy today. Just pack up anything that comes through online."

"Will do," Sorina agrees. She enjoys organizing, the practice soothing her mind, even if it sometimes means crawling around on her hands and knees in the back corners, but she wants to save her energy for tonight. "See you Sunday then?"

Jenelle nods. "You have anything exciting planned for your day off tomorrow?"

Sorina shakes his head, "Nah. Just going to get some things done. The usual." She imagines Jenelle's expression if she told her boss what she would be doing after work tonight.

The cage. I hope it's the cage. He said I could if I was good. I've been so, so good.

"Really?" Jenelle asks, a small frown on her lips. "You should go out, have a good time, a young girl like you. You should have some fun in this city, have a night on the town!"

Sorina laughs, wondering what Jenelle's idea of a night on the town is. Her own involves leather cuffs and blindfolds, strangers and that electric excitement of being at their mercy. "Maybe," she says.

Jenelle rolls her eyes. "You're only young once, you know. Trust me. I should have had more fun when I was your age."

"Then I'll try to have enough fun for both of us," Sorina offers. "Maybe I'll go to the park or something."

Jenelle shakes her head, retrieving her purse from beneath the counter and logging out of the computer. "I'll see you Sunday," she says as Sorina logs in, officially taking over the store for the day. After her boss leaves, Sylvia pulls out the paperback stashed in her bag and rests it on the counter.

It's a classic kind of day, so she heads into the store to find something traditional to match.

Chapter Two

Sorina is taking a break from her book to stretch her legs, walking the store and straightening the few out of place items, her need for perfect organization kicking in hard, when her phone chimes. The chime is a message from Dylan, and she scurries back to the counter to check it. Other messages can be ignored, like calls from her mother or texts from her few friends, but Dylan must be answered immediately.

5:45 pm [Dylan: Are you alone?]
5:45 pm [Sorina: Yes, Master.]
5:46 pm [Dylan: Go where no one on the street can see you.]

Sorina looks around the small store, settling on the empty space in the back behind the center aisle of records. It's her best chance of semi-privacy without going into the bathroom. But Dylan hadn't said the bathroom. He'd just said to avoid the street. She stands in the small area at the back of the store, scanning the two glass windows that overlook the street. They are covered with posters and advertisements, but the glass still has a few clear spaces where someone could peer inside. The bottom of the door is definitely clear, but the top is covered by their store hours and a few announcements.

She's fairly sure that anyone looking in would only see her head anyway, the rest hidden by the shelving.

5:47 pm [Sorina: I'm here. They can see my head if they look inside but nothing else.]
5:47 pm [Dylan: Good girl. Now put your hand up your shirt and squeeze your nipple through your bra.]

Low heat pools in Sorina's belly, and she rests the phone on the edge of the display, hand slowly skidding up the sensitive skin of her stomach, over the pink lace bra he chose for her, and she squeezes her nipple softly.

5:48pm [Dylan: Lift up your shirt. Pull your breast free from the bra. Lick your nipple, then blow on it.]

Sorina grins, looking around the store even though she knows there aren't any cameras in here. Jenelle wouldn't know how to work them even if she did own them. She lifts her shirt slowly anyway, rolling it above her breasts, then lifts one out as instructed, the weight heavy in her hand as she bends down to lick her nipples. She can't actually suck her nipple, which is what she wants to do, but she can lick the general area. Her double Ds make it easy to reach. She waits a moment, then blows, the cool air on her wet skin causing her to tremble, the hair on her arms standing on end.

"Mmm," she moans, a shiver racing through her. She drops her breast and reaches for the phone.

5:50 pm [Sorina: Yes, Master. Thank you, Master. What next, sir?]
5:50 pm [Dylan: Slide your fingers into your pants and feel yourself. Don't unbutton them. Tell me how wet you are.]

Sorina obeys, eager finger sliding between her waistband and her skin, dipping beneath the line of her matching pink panties to slide over her newly smooth skin. Another of Dylan's orders—get waxed for tonight. She smiles, the zing of pleasure shooting through her at the touch, and she removes her finger, the tip glistening with moisture. She reaches for the phone again.

5:51 pm [Sorina: Juicy, sir.]
5:51 pm [Dylan: Taste yourself. Tell me how you taste.]

Sorina slides her finger between her lips, savoring the taste on her tongue, wondering when Dylan will let her lick a pussy again. She loves cock, his cock—any cock, really—but pussy is still fascinating, all smooth and silky—the few she's licked anyway. Her nipples harden at the memory.

5:53 pm [Sorina: Like honey, sir. Sweet and musky.]
5:54 pm [Dylan: Unbutton your pants. Push them down your legs to your ankles. Leave the panties on but push them aside. Finger yourself. Hard. Fast. I expect you to come when I send my next message.]

Sorina puts the phone back down, resting it on top of the records in front of her, unbuttons her pants, and glances quickly at the street. She can see a few shapes on the sidewalk outside, but no one slows or touches the door. She yanks her pants down, feeling the cool air of the store on her bare legs, and that low pull in her belly twinges, pleasure spiraling out from her core at the idea of being so exposed at work.

Anyone can see me right now. Anyone at all.

Her hand drifts down to her panties, moving them aside as instructed, and she slides a finger inside, forgoing the pleasure of her clit to obey her master. It feels good, and she recalls his instructions: Hard. Fast. A second finger joins the first, then she uses her other hand to press hard against her clit as she moves her hand furiously. She squeezes tight around herself, the friction maddening. It's nice, but she knows that even if she comes, she will still want more, still want a cock to fill that space. Coming on fingers is good, but never great. Still, the thought of being naked and masturbating in the open like this at work is enough to add an edge, and her body tightens. She is dangerously close to the edge, but she knows she must wait for permission.

Wait, she commands herself. *Wait....wait for...*

It's too much. The naughtiness. The public display. All of it. She comes hard, shuddering on her fingers. An instant later, her phone buzzes.

5:58 pm [Dylan: Come for me, Sorina. Come now.]

Already there, sir.

She stands there for a moment before responding, the tiny act of rebellion making her smirk.

5:59 pm [Sorina: Thank you, sir.]
5:59 pm [Dylan: That was fast, Sorina. Very fast.]

Sorina bites her lip, guilt surging through her on the heels of her pleasure.

6:00 pm [Dylan: Did you wait for me, Sorina? Were you a good girl?]

Standing with her pants around her ankles and her shirt tucked above her boobs, Sorina stares down at her phone, a wave of heat flooding her, and not from the orgasm.

I can lie. He won't know. But I will know. Besides, he may punish me...

The prospect is enough to make her decide for truthfulness.

6:01 pm [Sorina: I am sorry, Master. I tried.]

Three long minutes pass, and Sorina makes no move to cover herself, occasionally glancing at the door to make sure she is still alone.

6:04 pm [Dylan: I am very disappointed, Sorina. I will have to punish you later. Get dressed and go back to work.]

She stares at the message, contemplating a response, but she sets it down on the albums with a sigh, bending down to pull up her pants. She has just finished putting herself to rights and walked back behind the counter when the door swings open, a handsome blonde man entering.

"Hey," she greets, taking a sip of her water bottle. Her hand smells like her pussy, and she hasn't had a chance to wash it yet. She will after the customer leaves.

He nods at her, a soft smile crossing his lips, and Sorina wonders what it would be like to kiss those lips. He seems vaguely familiar, but she can't place him. *Maybe he's come into the store before?*

She studies him as he walks down the opposite aisle, deft fingers flipping through the Ds. He reminds her of a hipster without the hat—plaid button-down shirt, dark jeans, shoulder-length hair, and a scruffy goatee that she wants to touch. She lets him skim for a while, watching the way he holds his body, the way he moves his hands, deciding that she wants to know what sounds he makes when he comes. *If only he'd come in a few minutes earlier, he'd have gotten quite a show...*

She glances at her phone, knowing she is supposed to text Dylan for permission any time she wants to fuck someone. She's allowed, of course. He wouldn't say no. But she's already disobeyed him by coming too soon, and if she asks now, he may deny her as punishment.

Sorina likes being punished—but she also likes coming on a hard cock—and right now, she wants this stranger in the store. She leans forward on the counter, propping her book up before her, knowing that if he glances over, he will see the outline of her ass in her jeans. A quick glance shows that he has been watching her, a little look here and there as he works his way through the three rows of Ds. When he begins skimming through the Es, she speaks.

"Help you find anything?" Her voice is low, sultry, and she gives him direct eye contact, loving how he meets her gaze. She narrows her eyes at him. "Let me guess: Depeche Mode?"

His smile reaches his eyes, and he tilts his head. "That obvious, huh?"

She shrugs. "I've worked here a while. We don't have anything from them in stock, but I can order it if you want." She pauses, then adds, "Looking for anything else?"

"How about the Bloodhound Gang?" he asks, a wicked smile teasing his lips.

"You looking for a little 'Bad Touch'?" she teases, hoping he follows her thoughts. The song is older, but his eyes light up in recognition.

He abandons the records, making his way around the aisle to stand in front of her. "That depends," he says, raising an eyebrow. "You up for some Discovery Channel?"

Sorina grins, putting her book down on the counter. "I don't know," she says, coming out from behind the counter, walking over to the Bs. The stranger follows her, and when she pauses, fingers flipping through the albums to reach the Bloodhound Gang, he steps up close behind her, body pressing against hers, soft breath on her neck. Sorina pushes back into him, her ass gently wiggling against his cock, pleased when she feels a sudden hardening press against her.

"Will we do it doggie style so we can both watch X-Files?" she sings, following the rhythm as she leans back into him, turning her face so his mouth finds hers, his lips soft. His hand grabs her hip and tugs her back against him even tighter, the other tangling in her hair. She moans at the pressure on her scalp, loving the way he moves her head around without asking.

The hand on her hip crawls up to cup her breast, and Sorina returns the favor, her hand snaking behind her to cup his cock through the jeans. He makes a muffled sound against her mouth, his tongue forcing its way deeper, and his hand slides down her body and into her jeans, bypassing her panties to press hard against her clit. Sorina almost comes right there at the stranger's touch, but then she remembers where they are. It's not like she hasn't fucked anyone at work before, but she's usually more careful. Then again, she's not always as worked up as she is right now, the fingering episode leaving her hungry for more action. Opening her eyes, she glances at the street. People hurry by outside, shadowy outlines in the late afternoon light, but no one enters.

The stranger's hand in her pants begins to move, fingers sliding back and forth across her clit, and she shudders, sensation swallowing her for a moment. She moans into his mouth, on the edge of orgasm again. She needs him inside of her.

Now.

He breaks the kiss to whisper against her lips, "Where?"

Sorina considers the end of the aisle again, but she doesn't want to risk leaning against the records and knocking anything over. He's taller than she is, so standing is definitely a possibility, but she's also wearing jeans, so even pulling them down will limit her range of motion. She doesn't want to risk taking them off completely, not while they are in the store.

Why didn't I wear a dress? The thought is fleeting—dresses at work are impractical given the amount of time she spends crawling around on the floor, though different clothing would make encounters like this one much easier.

She contemplates locking the door for a few minutes but decides against it. Another little rebellion, like not texting Dylan about her new friend. He's going to punish her so hard for this later tonight.

She can't wait.

"Behind the counter," she says after a moment, and he nods, stepping away from the rack of records, turning her body in front of his, and marching her around the counter. He leans her forward, her hands pressing against the glass top, then drags her jeans over her hips. She looks over her shoulder at him, watching his face as he appreciates the pink panties, then he smacks her ass, and she jolts forward, the shock blossoming into waves of pleasure.

"Oh yeah," she mumbles. "Like that!"

He grins, one hand working at the button of his jeans as the other winds up for another smack. She grunts at the impact, that warm flush vibrating though her, and she reaches around to help, pulling down his zipper and shorts in one quick tug, revealing a sizable hard cock. "Inside me," she demands. "Now."

"Yes, ma'am," he replies, then pushes her panties aside, sheathing himself in one hard stroke. Sorina cries out, both hands pressed flat against the counter to brace herself, but then he grabs one hand and tugs it behind her back, pressing it hard against her hip as he rocks into her again.

"God yes!" she cries as he thrusts again, but when she tries to push back against him, setting the rhythm hard and fast, he grabs her other hand and presses both against her back. Her breasts press hard into the countertop, the cool glass sliding against her rucked-up shirt. "More," she moans, loving the restraints while also wanting to move her body against his. The denied desire only drives her need for more—of everything. "More!" she demands.

The stranger moves behind her, three quick hard strokes pumping in and out. "More what?" he croons.

"More of that cock!" she demands, struggling to push back into him without her arms.

"Such a demanding girl," the stranger grunts, pounding into her with more force. He swats her ass again with his free hand, then digs his fingers into her hip and yanks her back to him. Sorina hopes she will have bruises tomorrow, a record of this chance encounter imprinted on her body. The idea is enough to send her shooting over the edge, and she shudders against him, squeezing tight as she comes. "Fuck yes," he groans, fucking her harder and faster. "Come on my cock again!" he demands, setting a brutal pace. Sorina squeals, the sound erupting out of her as she gets exactly what she wanted earlier when she fingered herself in the aisle. She looks up, watching the people on the street, wondering if her cries carry through the door. No one seems to notice, and she giggles at the naughtiness of it all—the public sex with a complete stranger...without texting Dylan first.

He's going to punish me so hard! The thought drives her over the cliff again, and she shudders against the stranger's cock, feeling him deep inside of her as he pumps harder. "Yes!" she cries. "Oh god yes!" The stranger releases her hip, grabbing her long ponytail of hair instead, twisting her head back as he yanks on it, pulling him into him with each thrust. "Yes fuck yes!" she yells again, not caring who hears her. The stranger pumps harder, hips shivering as he comes, his body leaning over on top of hers, both of them gasping for breath on top of the counter.

Oh yeah, Sorina thinks. *Tonight is going to be awesome.*

Chapter Three

At 9:58 that night, Sorina stands in her living room, proud of herself for being ready not only on time—but actually early. She still wears the pink bra and panties, but she traded her work jeans and t-shirt for a pink dress. The thigh high stockings were a last-minute addition, something to distract Dylan from the day's indiscretions, and she knows he will approve.

I hope he lets me go in the cage tonight.

They've been going to the sex club for months now, and while they have participated in several satisfying scenes, what Sorina really craves is time locked in the small cage, handcuffed and blindfolded while anyone can do anything to her. The blindfold makes it easy to give up control. If she can't see what's happening around her, she can't be paralyzed by indecision. She can let the moment swallow her, giving in to pure sensation, reveling in the ecstasy her body can provide.

At 10pm exactly, her front door opens. She turns to see Dylan striding inside, and something inside leaps at the sight of him, those long limbs, strong body, dark hair that catches the light just so. She had expected a text telling her to come downstairs and get in the car. Seeing him in her apartment means that her punishment will come sooner rather than later.

"Sorina," he says, and his voice makes her shiver. She loves hearing her name in his mouth. "You look perfect."

She dips her head, nodding in appreciation. "Thank you, Master."

He crosses the room, taking her in his arms and kissing her softly, gently. Sorina shivers, losing herself in his touch, knowing that while her master can be tender, he can also be wicked, and moments like these only enhance her excitement at what's coming. Breaking the kiss, he looks tenderly into her eyes. "Did you misbehave today, Sorina?" he whispers.

A chill runs through her. *Does he know about Tobin?* She'd learned her mystery lover's name before he left that evening. They'd exchanged numbers and made loose plans to meet again—preferably somewhere with a bed, he'd said. Dylan's face gives nothing away, and perhaps he is only referring to her minor indiscretion of coming without permission.

Well, minor in comparison to fucking someone without permission, of course. It's not cheating, not like that—she and Dylan are free to have sex with whomever they want whenever the occasion presents itself—but he ordered her to always ask first. This was partly another way of controlling her, freeing her from decision-making, but it was also about her safety. Sorina has fucked strangers in dangerous situations, only realizing afterward how easily the scene could have turned against her. Dylan promised to keep her safe—and texting is just another way of watching over her.

A tiny sliver of guilt works its way into her heart. *He's only trying to take care of me. I should let him.*

"I did," she replies, voice neutral as she looks away.

There is a long pause, but Sorina doesn't dare meet his gaze, knowing that he will ask her what she did. She won't lie to him, but if she can avoid mentioning Tobin until after she gets to spend time in the cage, she will. Finally, Sorina's nerve breaks, and she looks up at him. He raises an eyebrow, clearly deciding something, then he tuts his tongue. "So you did. And what do you think I should do about that?"

Sorina bites her lip, wondering what delightful punishment he has thought of. "I think you should punish me," she says quietly.

"Oh yes, and I will," he promises. "But how?"

This is new territory and something in Sorina's chest tightens at the question. The whole point of this relationship is that he relieves her of the burden of making choices. Having her choose her punishment breaks the rules in a terrible way. He must see the panic on her face because he speaks again.

"Don't you worry," he tells her. "I have something special worked out for tonight." He reaches down to put a hand inside one of his pockets, pulling out what look like thick rubber bands. "But first, let's get this settled." He kneels before her, a tap on the back of one leg the sign that she should put her heeled foot on his thigh. She watches as he slides her foot through one of the rubber bands, then proceeds to roll it up her leg to rest against her thigh, just at the top of her stockings. At her confused expression, he reaches between the band and her skin with one finger, a quick flick, and the band snaps back against her thigh. A sharp twang of pain lashes through her, and she jerks back, only Dylan's hands on her legs keeping her steady. She's never thought of rubber bands as a punishment before. She switches legs, allowing him to work the other band up her leg, settling it in place next to the other one. The top of her stocking offers some relief from the pinch and sting as he snaps it, but not a lot. She will have welts very soon.

Sorina expects him to put her foot back on the floor and stand, but instead, he glides his hands up her legs, taking a moment to snap both bands as he passes them, curling his hands around her ass beneath the dress. She lets herself lean into him, and he ducks his head beneath the skirt of her dress, breath hot against her skin. One hand traces the curve of her hip, and then he is sliding her panties down, just a little, enough to give him free access to her clit.

His tongue is warm heaven as he licks her, and she sinks even more into him, but then a snap of the rubber band brings her out of the moment—and quickly into another kind of headspace.

"What did I say, Sorina?" he whispers, breath hot against her sensitive skin. "Remind me of what you were supposed to do."

Sorina shudders against him as he licks her again, fingers sliding against her skin in the way he knows she loves. "I...I was supposed to wait," she manages.

"You weren't a very good girl, Sorina," he tells, alternating a sweet lick with another snap, the pleasure and pain a delicious contrast. "You were a greedy girl. Are you a greedy girl?"

"I'm sorry, Master," she breathes, reaching below her dress to tangle her hands in his hair.

He looks up at her, eyes disappointed. "Where is my obedient Sorina?" he asks.

"I'm here, Master," she assures him. "I will obey you." She is rewarded by a long series of perfect pressure on her clit matched by sweet sliding fingers inside of her. "Oh, please..." she moans, close to the edge.

"Please what?" he encourages, returning to that sweet rhythm.

"Please let me come, Master!"

He rewards her words with a savage snap of both bands, and the heat in her belly explodes. She shudders against him, body reeling with release. "Thank you!" she gushes, hands pressing him hard against her. "Thank you!"

After sliding her panties back up to her hips, he leans back to look up at her, a lazy grin on his face. "I love watching you come," he says. "I can't wait to see you tonight."

Sorina bites her lip. "Is... tonight the night?" she whispers.

Dylan nods, then stands, taking both of her hands. "Let's go," he says.

Chapter Four

Dylan blindfolds her before they go inside the club, so Sorina has no real sense of the space around her. She's been inside before, though, so she remembers that the cage is near the entrance, situated so everyone walking inside can see the person inside. It's a small cage, maybe three feet across, with thin bars made for arms and legs to fit through easily—the better to tease the person inside. The cage is tall, and the cross bar across the top, intended to clip to cuffs or chains, can be moved up and down so the person can stand or sit inside.

He helps her inside. Sorina can hear the soft mumble of people talking, and Dylan greets several others as they head into the big room. She can feel the eyes on her, but she can't see anything but the velvety blackness in front of her, and the feeling is sublime. She allows herself to be led around, Dylan's strong hands on her hips and the small of her back as they move.

"Wait here," he orders, and Sorina obeys, standing as he instructed, her hands hanging loose at her sides. She can hear shuffling, movement, and she senses bodies nearby, but no one touches her. After a long moment, Dylan speaks again, his voice close to her ear. "Lift your arms," he tells her. Sorina obeys, and he lifts the dress over her head, the silky material sliding off her arms, her hair slipping down to touch her bare back. She wonders if she should pull her hair back, but then Dylan is touching her wrists, buckling the leather cuffs into place. He tugs her forward, and she steps over a small threshold, the ground beneath her high heels metal but with slight bumps all over. Sorina imagines the diamond plate she's seen in factory floors, meant to allow people to keep their grip on the otherwise smooth surface. Her cuffed hand is raised above her head, and she hears the snick of the other end clicking into place. Another cuff touches her other hand, the velvet interior soft against her skin, and it too is raised above her head. Her hands have enough space to move side to side, though no more than the length of the cuff allows. Dylan moves away from her, and she hears the sound of a door swinging shut, the metal clang followed by sounds of locks sliding into place.

She examines her new space, pushing her arms out to test her range of motion. She's definitely cuffed to a point above her, probably in the center of the cage, but she can pull down far enough to bend her elbows, though she brushes against the cool metal bars of the cage if she does. Her legs are free, and she pushes her foot out slowly, heels dragging along the metal floor with a low scuffing noise, and she finds the edge of the cage. Her foot can fit between the bars, but only up to her shin, at which point the bars are too close together to move any more.

Without her sight, she focuses on her other senses—the low music in the background, something wordless with a slow sultry beat making her want to sway her hips if she listens to it too long. She can smell leather and the quiet bite of clean metal, her own deodorant and musky perfume wafting as her skin heats.

I wonder who is watching me right now. If anyone. I could be alone in this room and I wouldn't know.

But she knows that she isn't alone. She can hear the quiet voices around her, the low thud of someone being paddled, the soft moan of satisfaction. It's still early in the night, but she knows that soon those moans will get louder, more pervasive as the patrons loosen up and really unwind. This a private club: no phones, no evidence, and no rules beyond consent. Sorina wonders if a stranger will fuck her tonight, if it's possible through the bars.

Tobin's face drifts through her mind, and she hopes she will see him again. He was delightful. The thought makes her wonder about Dylan—*does he know?* The rubber bands on her legs are certainly punishment, but they are for coming too soon. If he wanted to really punish her, he wouldn't let her in the cage with the blindfold on. He knows that's what she really craves—the anonymity of being captive and at everyone's mercy while unable to see who is touching her.

A hand traces along her thigh, and Sorina stiffens, not expecting the touch. The touch becomes a hand, the palm cupping her right thigh, and then someone snaps the rubber band around her other thigh, and she shudders. The hand moves up her thigh, over the line of her panties and pauses again on the soft skin of her stomach. Another finger glides along her shoulder, and Sorina wonders if they belong to the same person.

Maybe it's Dylan. Maybe not. Dylan likes to watch, will probably spend the whole night just watching other people touch her—only having his way with her at the very end, so he is the last one to claim her. The hand on her belly slides up to cup a breast, and Sorina bites her lip, hoping it will move to squeeze her nipple. A sudden snap of the rubber band shocks her, and she jerks away, moving back, and the hand cupping her breast twists to reach inside, pinching her nipple just as another hand touches her chin, running along her jawline, before slipping a finger inside her mouth. She sucks it in, trying to identify what she can. Probably a man, by the tough feel of the skin around the nail. It tastes faintly of soap, but not in a bad way, and she rotates her tongue around it, mimicking the motion she uses for a dick. There is a gasp nearby, someone enjoying himself, and another hand touches her lower leg, sliding up her calf as the hand in her bra continues to massage her nipple.

Definitely different people, she thinks, losing herself to sensation.

The first few touches are sweet, exploratory, but then one hand settles on her side and wiggles as if to tickle her. Sorina jerks back with a hiss, nearly biting the finger in her mouth, and a voice says, "Oh, yes. Tickle her." Sorina bites her lip in preparation. She doesn't enjoy tickling, hates the way her body reacts without her control, but here, trapped in the cage, blindfolded, handcuffed, and at a stranger's mercy, she gives herself over the feeling, giggling madly as the hand continues its relentless movement, hating the sensation even as she loves the release it offers. She is keenly aware of her body as a body, her sensitive skin over her bones teased as those questing fingers continue to explore every inch of her, seeking an even more ticklish spot. Fingers torment her armpits while others tickle her sides.

She still wears her heels, her bare feet protected from tickle torture. A hand wraps around her ankle, clearly intending to remove her shoe, but Dylan's quiet command stops the movement. His face must say something, because there are no more words, but the tickling focuses on the exposed parts of her body instead, and no one tries to take off her shoes. It's a tiny relief, a small part of herself that remains her own, safe from the abuse, though the rest of her enjoys the release of giving into the indignities of her skin, the snorting shrieks that escape her lips as she tries to twist away, only to find more tickling hands behind her.

Slowly, the tickles slow down, morphing into something more fluid, the touches on her skin sensual rather than teasing, and Sorina's skin sparks in response. She leans into the touches, body conflicted about which direction she wants to move. The hand on her stomach trails down to dip inside her panties while the hand on her shoulder dips down to pinch her nipple. Another hand snaps the band on her thigh, while yet another squeezes her ass. Sorina leans back, her body pressing into the cold bars behind her, and someone kisses a line up her neck, sliding her hair over her shoulders to trail over her breasts. Another hand finds its way into her panties from behind, fingers dipping between her cheeks to circle her asshole. She sighs, pressing back into the touch, and then her arms are being lowered, the hands encouraging her to her knees. Sorina obeys, hands still held above her head, but now with plenty of room for her to kneel. The metal floor bites into her skin, and she bites her lip, the dull ache welcome against the sharp snap along her thighs as someone snaps the band again. She flattens her feet in the heels, the top of her foot resting on the floor and reminds herself to stay upright so she doesn't spike herself accidentally. Her thighs will already be a mess tomorrow—she doesn't want to add a scrape from heels to the party.

That's not the kind of pain she wants anyway.

Hands gently touch her face, more fingers pressing against her lips, seeking entrance, and then she is sucking on them. These are smaller fingers, delicate, and the smooth nails suggest polish or gel—maybe a woman's hands? The fingers coax her forward, mouth following along, and then something else is before her lips. She recognizes the cock immediately, enjoys how the hand on her face seems to guide the cock into her mouth. She leans forward eagerly, circling the tip with her tongue and wrapping her lips around it, sucking a little to pull it closer. It doesn't move, the owner probably pressed up against the bars, so she leans forward more, her arms tugging on the cuffs as she reaches the edge of her reach. More hands stroke her head, tugging her hair out of the way as she sucks more of the cock in her mouth. She wonders whose cock it is, whether it's another stranger or someone she knows, and she listens hard, ears straining for the sounds of heavy breathing she knows she must be eliciting from her partner.

Instead, she gasps as two hands pull her back by her hips, her butt pressed up against the bars as a hand moves her panties aside and runs along her slit. Another hand works around her front, rubbing her clit in rhythmic circles while the other hand continues to run up and down her opening. She groans, sucking harder on the cock in her mouth, and pushes back into the hands. Another hand reaches inside her bra and pinches her nipple while yet another snaps the band on her thigh. She squeals, the sensations flooding her, the warm heat in her belly pooling and rising through her center. The pressure on her clit continues, and soon she is sliding over the edge, her body tightening with release. Fingers weave their way through her hair, seemingly connected to the cock in her mouth, and Sorina sucks harder, tugging the stranger over the edge with her. Cum fills her mouth, and she swallows reflexively. The cock hovers for a moment, the hands still tight on her head, but then they release, and the cock slips out of her mouth.

She pauses for a moment, catching her breath, but the hands return to her panties, this time sliding them down over her ass to hover around her thighs. The fingers become more insistent, sliding inside of her while another hand restarts those small circles on her clit. She moans, licking her lips, and then another cock is pressing against her cheek, a trail of cum leaving wetness across her skin before the head finds her mouth.

At the same time, the fingers inside of her move aside, migrating to circle her asshole instead as a hard cock presses against her opening. Sorina squeals with glee, pressing her ass hard against the bars, giving the cock more access to her pussy, and the head slips between her lips, just pressing gently inside of her opening. The cock in her mouth surges forward at the same time, and two new hands cup her breasts, pulling them free of the bra and squeezing her nipples in tandem with the cock pulsing in her mouth and the other teasing her opening.

Oh fuck yes!

She presses back again, wanting to encourage the cock behind her, but the cage prevents her from claiming him. Her hands flail against the cuffs with a metal clang as she tries to move her body and control the motion, demanding more.

"Oh no, Sorina," Dylan's voice coos nearby. "You don't get to set the rules here. You just get to experience it. Let it happen."

Sorina's body relaxes instantly, sagging into the hands around her, the soft feel of manicured nails running through her hair while she sucks the cock in her mouth slowly, enjoying the feel of the soft warm skin against her tongue. The cock barely in her pussy slides forward slowly, a tiny fraction at a time, and the fingers massaging her asshole slide inside just a little bit. The hand on her clit continues to rub in steady circles, and Sorina feels another orgasm building inside.

She can hear heavy breathing around her, and the telltale slap of hands on cocks, and she wonders who is jerking off nearby. An image forms in her mind, a circle of men standing all around the cage, all with their dicks in hand, jerking off as they watch the stranger fuck her from behind while she sucks the other man's cock. The idea is enough to make her nipples harden again, her core tightening, and she shudders again, body expanding in pleasure.

The cock inside her begins to move in earnest, filling her pussy more with each stroke. The cock in her mouth twitches, and Sorina knows he is close. She uses her teeth a little, nibbling along the head just a touch, and the cock twitches even more. If she didn't have a cock in her mouth, Sorina would smile.

The hands squeeze her nipples again, and hands grip her hips, holding her immobile against the cage as the cock plows in and out. Her knees ache, and then someone snaps the bands on her thighs, and the pain streaks through her like a brand, and she comes harder, body jerking as the waves of pleasure wash her away. The cock in her mouth explodes, shooting warm cum down her throat, and the cock in her pussy pumps hard two, three more times before filling her with warmth, the hands gripping her hips hard. At the same moment, warm patches of heat strike her skin all over, the men around the cage coming in a round circle of release.

The cock in her mouth pulls away, and Sorina licks her lips, body singing in satisfaction. She is completely in the moment, completely content in herself.

Then Dylan enacts her punishment.

Hands tug the blindfold from her head. She is blinded for a moment, the dim lights of the club too bright for her sensitive eyes, but soon enough, the world swims back into focus. She stares through the bars of the cage to see Tobin standing in front of her, a perfect smile on his face. Dylan stands next to him, a hand on his shoulder.

Sorina glances madly around, panic swirling through her at the sight of so many people leaning against the cage, some with hands still reaching between the bars to touch her. Many of the men have their cocks out, and she glances behind her, wondering which of the three men standing back there was just fucking her. She vaguely recognizes some familiar faces, but no one she has played with before. Shame fills her, and even as it does, part of her rejoices at the sensation, the humiliation of being locked in this cage and covered with strangers' cum. She turns her head forward again, looking up into Dylan's face.

"Is there something you want to tell me, Sorina?" Dylan croons, kneeling down so his face is level with hers. "Something you'd like to confess?"

"I..." Sorina stalls, not sure what to say. Tobin stands there, perfectly comfortable, so clearly he's in on it. She wants to be annoyed with him, but she can't find the feeling. Instead, she wants him to fuck her again, this time with Dylan and everyone else watching. "I may have forgotten to text you, Master," she mumbles.

"What was that, Sorina?" he prompts, a hand stroking her cheek, scooping up a stray line of cum and sliding it into her mouth.

She swallows, then repeats herself in a louder voice. "Forgive me," she adds.

"And here I sent you a gift," Dylan says, shaking his head, "knowing how much you like to be fucked after fingering yourself. I knew you would want more, and Tobin here was quite eager to make your acquaintance, especially after what he saw last time we were here."

Sorina bites her lip. *So, that's why he was familiar*, she thinks.

"Tell me, Sorina, how was he?" Dylan purrs. "Did you enjoy my gift?"

"He was amazing," she says honestly. "So good."

Dylan nods approvingly. "I'm glad to hear it. Unfortunately, you're going to have to wait until you've been properly punished before you get to enjoy him again."

Chapter Five

Dylan approaches and unlatches the cage door. He reaches inside, carefully avoiding her body. When Dylan unhooks her cuffs from the bar overhead, he tugs gently, and she gets clumsily to her feet. She stumbles, and several people reach through the bars to steady her, their fingers an odd mixture of hot and cold, smooth and clammy, as they help her to her feet.

Pins and needles slowly work their way down her lower legs, the top of her feet burning as sensation pours back into her. She sways dangerously, and Dylan collects her in his arms, tugging her close before he swings her body up against his chest, lifting her out of the cage. She sags against him, hardly noticing when one high heel thumps to the metal floor of the cage. She snuggles absently into his chest, relishing the security of his closeness, knowing that her reprieve is only temporary, that she still needs to be properly punished.

The idea sparks something deep within, and she smiles, twisting her face away from his chest to take in the room around her. Dylan carries her away from the cage to a bench set beneath another length of chain suspended from the ceiling. Sorina notes the empty ring at the bottom, perfectly placed to cuff her to, keeping her arms above her head. Her shoulders already ache from being in that position, but she's excited to repeat the posture, especially being able to see her partners, knowing that without the cage between them, anyone will be able to touch her in any way they want.

A shiver runs through her, and Dylan looks down, nodding when he sees that she is recovered and ready for the next round. He gives her a soft, secret smile meant only for her, then sets her down on the bench, one leg on each side. His hands run down the length of her legs as he lets her go, but he snaps one of the rubber bands with a wink before lifting her arms above her head again and attaching the cuffs to the chain above. He steps back, allowing a woman and Tobin to take his place. The woman is lovely, a petite brunette with bouncy curls surrounding her face, and she bites her lip as she sits in front of Sorina.

"You are so sexy," she says quietly, reaching up to push Sorina's hair behind an ear. "May I kiss you?"

Sorina nods, leaning forward to meet her new friend's soft lips. The kiss is gentle, sweet, and another pair of hands begins to rub Sorina's shoulders from behind. She glances down, opening her eyes to study the fingers and recognizes Tobin's big hands. He rubs hard, easing the sore muscles of her shoulders before sliding over to work her neck, fingers running through her hair and along her scalp. The woman runs a hand up from Sorina's waist, brushing along the edge of her bra, and she looks down at it, a question in her eyes. Sorina nods, glad that Dylan chose a bra with removable straps so that when Tobin unclips the back, she can tug the straps free and pull the bra completely away, instead of it lingering around her arms and head somewhere above her. The woman bends her head down, taking Sorina's nipple into her mouth, and Sorina moans, the warm heat thrilling. She's had many men suck her nipples, but there is something different about a woman's mouth, the fullness of her lips, the gentle press of her tongue, that makes the heat pool in Sorina's belly.

Tobin's hands begin sliding down her back to rest on her hips, and she pushes back into him, trying to get a sense of where his body is without looking away from the woman nuzzling her nipples.

"Oh, honey," the woman says, "I think I need to taste you." Sorina grins, and Tobin's hands on her hips lift her up off the bench just enough to slide her panties down. The woman takes them from her side, lifting one of Sorina's legs back over the bench so her legs are on the same side of the bench as her panties slide off her ankles. The woman runs both hands back up Sorina's legs, pausing the snap one of the rubber bands with a wicked wink, before she tugs the leg back over to the other side again, spreading Sorina wide and pressing her back on the bench. Sorina's arms move forward as her body lays back, the slack in the cuffs enough to let her dangle at a 45-degree angle from the bench. The movement changes the strain on her arms, and she sighs, enjoying the pull forward and up rather just straight up.

Tobin is sitting behind her, and her back lands against his bare chest. He leans down to nuzzle her neck, then moves over to claim her mouth. At the same time, the woman pushes forward, her warm breath teasing Sorina's clit, and she moans into Tobin's mouth. The woman has small deft fingers that she slides just inside, pressing up in a rhythm that matches her tongue on Sorina's clit. Pleasure explodes through Sorina, and her body tightens, hands jerking against the cuffs as she longs to run her fingers through the woman's hair, to hold her head, guiding this way and that. Not that the stranger needs much guidance, her skilled fingers and tongue bringing Sorina right to the edge and over in a matter of moments.

She screams into Tobin's mouth. The woman only pauses a moment, then continues her motion. A soft gasp against her skin makes Sorina open her eyes and look down. She grins, looking up to meet the man's eyes who has positioned himself behind her new friend, hard cock pressing against her. The woman looks over her shoulder, bobs her head in assent, then returns to her work between

Sorina's thighs. Her friend's hands and mouth continue to work beautifully, the rhythm now enhanced by the slow steady pulse of the man fucking her with long thrusts. He watches Sorina as he fucks the woman, biting his lip. He grips her hips, fucking her harder for a moment, then pauses to pull back and slap her ass. The woman bucks in pleasure, her mouth sucking hard on Sorina's clit, and she smiles at the stranger, eyefucking him while Tobin's hands slide down to pinch her nipples. Her body tightens, on the brink of release, and then she is coming hard.

The woman between her legs looks up, satisfaction on her face as she pushes back against the man fucking her and smiles. "I think I need you to sit on my face," she suggests, spinning around to put her back on the bench, looking up at Sorina expectantly. The man between her legs kneels so he can continue to fuck her, and Tobin helps Sorina stand up with one leg on either side of the bench. He tugs on the chain overhead, and it clicks up a few inches, allowing Sorina to stand with her arms overhead again. She hovers over the woman's face, her lipstick smudged around her full lips, shiny with Sorina's juices, and her new friend reaches out to wrap her arms around Sorina's hips, finding the same sweet spot with her tongue.

Sorina's head falls back in pleasure, and she closes her eyes for a moment, lost in sensation. She feels movement in front of her, and when she opens her eyes, Tobin is standing on the bench before her, pants unbuttoned and his cock just above the level of her mouth. She reaches for him, and the woman tightens her grip on her hips, tugging her down again. Sorina strains more, barely managing to lick the tip of Tobin's cock, her need for more growing with each determined suck between her legs. Tobin smiles above her where he holds the chain with one hand to keep himself steady. He bends his knees a little, allowing Sorina to suck his cock in her mouth in one desperate move, and she teases him with her tongue.

The moment is perfect: the mouth between her legs, the cock in her mouth, the eyes of the people watching their show, the sounds of fucking so close and yet not her own.

Not yet.

She is about to come again, then Tobin stands up straight, his cock slipping out of her mouth. She frowns, making a disappointed noise at his exit, but then his hands are in her hair again, wrapping it around his hand and pressing hard. A stranger snaps the band around her thigh and she jerks, her hair pulling tight against her scalp, and then she is coming again, savagely riding the woman's face. Tobin seems to sense her need because he tugs on the chain, letting her down again, but instead of allowing her to settle on the bench when the woman scoots down and sits up, her attention focused on the man fucking her now, Tobin sits beneath her, settling her on his lap, his hard cock pressed against her entrance.

"You want me down in your South Seas?" he quotes the Bloodhound Gang again, and Sorina laughs, pushing forward and onto him in one thrust. His hands curve around her hips and ass as he moves in her, setting a devastating rhythm. Sorina surrenders to him, surprised to find herself satisfied with just one partner, but relieved that she can focus on singular sensations at last—the touch of her hands on her ass, the press of his mouth against hers, the fullness of his cock sliding in and out of her pussy. The orgasm builds slowly despite the frenetic pace, and Tobin's hand returns to her hair, tugging her hair back. The glow in her belly ignites again.

"Look at me," he demands. "I want to watch you come on my cock, beauty."

Sorina obeys, coming hard and fighting to keep her eyes open to stare at him. He smiles at her, pleased, and when his eyes close for a moment, preparing for his own pleasure, Sorina glances over his shoulder to where Dylan stands a few feet away, face hungry as he watches her. She smiles at her master, pleased despite the punishment, knowing that while she loves the feeling of invisibility behind the blindfold, there is another part of her that thrives on exhibitions like this, and he has punished her with a reminder of that joy.

"Come for me," he mouths at her, and her body obeys, tightening around Tobin's cock as he grunts, coming for her, and they both slide over the edge together.

Oh yes, Sorina thinks, *punishment indeed.*

Chapter Six

Later, Dylan carries her into her apartment, setting her gently on the bed. He takes off her shoes, even the one reclaimed from the cage floor as they left the club. As he slides her stockings down, his touch is gentle, practical, but not sexual. Sorina is sensually exhausted, her body on the edge of endurance, wrung out from so many orgasms and the overload of touch and satisfaction. His fingers are extremely gentle as he removes the rubber bands, careful not to let them touch or pull her skin on the way down, fingers stretched out around her legs in a protective embrace. Her thighs have concurrent rings of red around them, welts that will surely sting even more when he gets her in the shower.

She knows that's where this is heading. Dylan often bathes her after a long night like this, her normally severe master quiet and soothing as he cleans her and puts her to bed. She raises her arms automatically to let him tug the dress free, though the motion makes her back and shoulders ache. He removes her bra and panties before leading her into the bathroom. He turns the water on, then quickly undresses as they wait for the water to heat up.

She is not so far gone that she doesn't appreciate the lines of his body as he stands naked before her, but his cock is only slightly hard, knowing that what she needs right now isn't more fucking.

When the water is warm, he helps her inside the shower stall, letting her stand beneath the spray as he begins to lather soap in his hands. He begins with her feet, washing them and sliding up her legs. He does not soap her thighs near the red welts, knowing that the burn will be too intense, settling for a thorough soaping of her ass and pussy instead. Her belly is next, and he massages her breasts with soap before finishing with her armpits and arms.

He shampoos her hair next, fingers massaging her scalp, then unhooks the shower head and sprays the remaining soap from her body. When he is finished, he uses the conditioner, running his fingers through her hair and finger combing the worst tangles, using the slippery cream to detangle as much as possible. He lets the conditioner sit for a moment, rubbing her shoulders and neck with his strong fingers.

When she sighs, leaning back against him, he rinses her a final time, careful to remove all of the soap and conditioner before turning off the water and wrapping her in a large towel. He slings a towel around his hips quickly, just to catch the dripping, then resumes his care, patting her dry with the towel and leading her back to the bed. He works on her hair, brushing it out with slow steady strokes, then stands up to pull out a nightshirt from her dresser. He returns to the bathroom with her towel to hang it up and comes back to kneel before the bed, a tube of first aid cream in one hand as he rubs the soothing cream over the welts on her legs. She will have bruises, but those don't require care.

He tugs the long shirt over her head, lifting her hair over the neck, then pulls the blankets down, settling her against the pillow and tucking the blanket over her. She can hear him moving around her apartment after that, but Sorina is barely aware of it. She does rouse when he lifts a straw to her lips, a soft command to drink making her turn her head enough to sip the water he has provided. He sets the water bottle on the nightstand, then continues moving around her apartment some more.

The next time Sorina opens her eyes, the lights are off, and he is getting into bed beside her, tucking her into his chest the way she likes. She snuggles into him, her master, safe and content in his arms.

In the middle of the night, he wakes her with soft kisses, making love to her with a gentleness that breaks the remains of her walls. His cock is hard inside of her, but he moves slowly, an easy rhythm that she sinks into, her body building to a release that surprises her in its intensity. She didn't think she had any more orgasms in her tonight, but Dylan proves her wrong, his touch soft but insistent. Gentle he may be—denied he would not. She knows that watching her with others excites him, and sometimes their fucking is intense and passionate. Other times, especially after nights like this, he lifts her back into the world of sensation with inexorable patience, and her body sings in release. It's not the same as the strong orgasms she has with strangers; it's something more soulful, and it's the reason why Dylan is the one who takes her home.

Satisfied in another way, Sorina drifts back into sleep with Dylan still on top of her, his softening cock still inside of her. In the morning, she is awakened by a familiar voice in her ear.

"Wake up Sorina," her master whispers.

Sexual Playground

HONEY POT COLLECTION

Ali Whippe

Dedication

For all the people who like to play

Chapter One

"Hey handsome," Emily croons into the phone, "you gonna be home soon to fuck me silly? I can't wait to play with you."

There is a pause, and her husband coughs. She can hear the sound of the car humming in the background, and then the tiny titter of her daughter's laughter. "Mommy said a bad word!" she whisper-shrieks. Her tone turns accusatory, "Are you and mommy going to the playground without us?!"

"You're on the car speaker," Ryan says, way too late to save her. "And mommy was just excited to hear from us!" he explains to their four-year old. "Sometimes mommy forgets to use her nice words when she gets excited." He pauses, then adds, "And no, we're not going to the playground without you. Grandma will definitely take you to their playground this weekend."

You fucker, she thinks. *Excited indeed.* "I'm sorry, Penny," Emily says gently. "Mommy was teasing Daddy." She pauses, then adds, her tone slightly acerbic, "I thought you would have dropped them off by now."

"That's why I called," her husband replies, a heavy sigh filling the pause. "We're sitting in traffic, and it looks like it's going to be a while. I didn't want you to get ready to go out and then have to wait forever for me to get home."

Emily nods, though she knows he can't see her, a habit she never managed to break.

"Are you nodding at me?" Ryan prompts.

Emily giggles, and she hears her daughter echo the sound, followed by a high-pitched squeal.

"Shh, pumpkin," Ryan soothes. "We don't want to wake your brother." Emily hears more shushing noises, but this time it's Penelope insisting that Oliver will sleep through anything. "Hey, honey," he says, distracted now as he prepares to hang up, "I just wanted to let you know."

"I can order in," Emily suggests, almost relieved to skip the restaurant. "What are you feeling?"

"I can pick something up on the way back," he offers. "Italian okay?"

"Perfect," Emily agrees, settling herself against the kitchen counter. "Okay, sweetie, be good for grandma and grandpa this weekend!"

"I will!" Penny promises. "Olly will be good, too, Mommy. I'll make sure of it."

"I know you will," Emily tells her, certain that their daughter will boss her little brother around the entire time.

"Talk to you soon," Ryan says. There is more of the hum from the car driving, then the call ends. Emily puts it down on the counter, eyes skipping to the clock on the oven.

5:46. If Ryan hasn't even gotten to his parents' house yet, he won't be home for a good hour or so. *A whole hour just for me,* she muses. *No husband. No kids. No chores.*

Well, yes, chores, but none that I'm going to do tonight. Thoughts of unwashed laundry, gritty floors, grimy sinks, and sticky counters flash across her mind, but she lets it all go, knowing her to-do list will still be there on Sunday when Ryan leaves to go get the kids. She can clean the house then. Now, however, her kid-free weekend has begun, and she won't let a moment of it go to waste.

She considers her options. *Empty house*, she muses. *All alone.* What to do first? Looking around at the kitchen, she takes in the few dishes stacked in the sink, evidence of the kids' snacks still lingering on the counter next to the fridge—the open bag of goldfish crackers and a few slices of apple still rest next to a small bowl of mostly eaten peanut butter. Her instinct is to clear the mess away, but this is her special weekend, and she forces herself to ignore it, hopping up on the counter above the dishwasher instead. This surface is clean, her tidy habits wiping down this side of the kitchen after lunch. Emily finds her attention wandering back to the goldfish and apples again, and she turns away.

I wonder... she glances at the clean counter behind where she sits, the granite countertop of the island extending behind the sink. On a whim, she lays back, relishing the feel of the cold surface as it sinks into her back, especially the bare skin of her neck and shoulders where her tank top doesn't cover. She straightens a bit, scooting so she lays behind the sink, her hair fanning out on the surface behind her. Instead of the mess on the other counter, she stares up into the pendulum lights that hang over this side of the island, lighting the eat-in bar they rarely use for anything but piling random stuff. The surface is clear today—Emily tidied while the kids napped—and she stretches to her full height, her hands dangling off the edge above her head as she wiggles, a grin crossing her face at the odd position.

Why haven't we had sex on this counter? She knows Ryan would be up for it—her husband is generally up for anything. She knows the answer—*because we have two small children.* The idea of getting busy on the counter is hot, but not when one of the kids stumbles downstairs into the kitchen, rubbing their sleepy eyes and asking what daddy is doing to mommy on the countertop.

They're managed to have sex in fun places around the house on those few weekends when Ryan's parents watch the kids, but they just never made it into the kitchen.

Note to self, Emily thinks. *This counter is probably a perfect height.* She pictures her husband: his long legs and broad shoulders, the look in his eye as he lifts her onto the countertop, that sexy confidence that first drew her to him back in college. First, he would push her back so she lay on the counter, her legs bent at the knee, feet dangling in front of the dishwasher, and he would slide her pants off.

Emily's hand drifts down her waist, following the curve of her stomach and slipping inside her pants. Biting her lip, she imagines Ryan leaning down to lick her pussy, his fingers slipping inside as he sucks on her clit. Her pants are tight, and while she sometimes enjoys the restriction, she doesn't want it now. She's alone. The house is hers, and if she wants to masturbate on the kitchen counter, she's going to do it without straining against her pants. She shimmies her hips, sliding her pants down her legs and kicking them off, letting them land on the kitchen floor. Her panties are next, joining her pants somewhere on the tile expanse, and she pauses, listening for the clack of the dog's nails on the floor. Hearing nothing, she settles back. Javert must still be zonked in his bed in the office. *Good,* she thinks. *He won't disturb me then. Nothing worse than opening my eyes to stare into a dog's soul when I'm getting busy.*

She returns to the fantasy, letting her fingers drift over her clit the way she imagines Ryan's tongue would nuzzle her body. A moan escapes her lips, and her eyes fly open, worried for a second that someone will hear, but then she remembers that she is alone, and she moans again just for the fun of it, reveling in the feeling. Her fingers speed up, and she feels that pull low in her belly. Her nipples tighten, the cold countertop making her thighs break out in gooseflesh as her fingers move faster, pressing in harder circles with each passing moment. Her free hand slides up and under her tank top, gripping her breasts and squeezing her nipples as she imagines Ryan pulling her closer to the edge, tongue feverishly sucking her clit while his fingers slide in and out of her.

"Oh yeah," she moans, heat building as she squirms on the counter, the only sound her panting breath and the wet sounds of her fingers rubbing her pussy. "Yes!" she shouts, the orgasm rushing over her with a warm wave of satisfaction. She lies there for a moment, hand pressed against her throbbing clit, soaking in the naughty feeling of masturbating on her kitchen counter.

More, she thinks. *I still have lots of time. I want to come at least three more times before Ryan gets back with dinner—and if things go as planned tonight, I'll get to come even more later on.*

Chapter Two

Emily sits naked on the couch in the living room, clothes abandoned on the kitchen counter—she did pick her pants and panties up off the floor—and scrolls through the porn available on her phone. She takes a few minutes to consider her options: ever-popular lesbians, hot nubile teens, point of view, threesomes, sexy massages, romantic encounters, gang bangs, office hookups... She passes the first three screens, then hops to the search bar, scrolling the categories. She watches porn with Ryan when they get the chance, but this time is just for her, so she searches for something just for her.

Hmmm, she thinks. *I'm home alone and can make noise, so definitely something loud. And with dirty talking,* she decides. *Really filthy talking. And more than two people.* Clicking both options, she scrolls the choices, settling on a short scene called "Lily and her Roommates: Group Sex, Fucking, Dirty Talk." She clicks the power for the TV, then darts upstairs while the system loads, snagging her vibrator from the drawer of sex toys in the closet. Looking over the choices, she picks up a small bullet as well, wanting both forms of stimulation. The other toys beckon—the vibrator with the attached hummingbird to touch her clit, the two-pronged dildo for pussy and ass, the sturdy dildo she uses when they pull out the

Rodeoh shorts and the strap-on and she pegs Ryan, the rolled-up restraints and bottles of lube—but she leaves them for the moment. Heading back down the stairs with her pussy and ass exposed to the room causes a rush of naughty heat to flood her belly—naked on the stairs! She reaches the couch, glad to see the video has loaded on the big screen, but is waiting for her to press play on her phone.

"Oh yeah," the big blonde on screen says, spreading her legs wide on a bed, "you'd better fuck me good, big boy!"

Emily chuckles, a hand reaching up to cup her breast and pinch her nipple, getting back into the mood. Her other hand slides down to stroke her pussy, fingers slow as she watches the scene.

Three men have entered the bedroom with the blonde—one kneeling to tug her legs to the edge of the bed so he can bury his face in her pussy. She moans, demanding, "Lick that pussy!" She turns to the tall man on her right, gesturing for him to come closer, then she wraps her hand around his cock, her perfect porn French manicured nails careful not to jab him as she starts jerking him off. The third man lays down on the bed on her other side, hands taking her face into his and begins kissing her passionately.

Emily reaches for the vibrator, pressing it against her opening, but not pushing inside, not yet, leaving the toy off for the moment, enjoying the teasing pressure of the cock-shaped silicone against her flesh.

"Fuck yes!" the woman on the screen yells, and the camera pans down to focus on the man between her legs, his tongue flicking madly against her clit, a hand sliding a finger inside her wet folds. Emily mimics the motion, pushing the tip of the vibrator inside of her.

The pressure almost makes her come immediately, and she shudders on the edge, pausing to let the moment shatter her slowly. When she can no longer wait, she turns on the bullet, pressing it to her clit. The orgasm rushes through her, her thighs trembling with her release.

"Fuck yes!" she yells to the empty house, screaming her pleasure the way she longs to do when she has sex with Ryan when the kids are home. She spends a lot of time muffling her shouts into pillows, biting her tongue, and forcing the sound of ecstasy back inside. The freedom to scream is intoxicating, and she moves the bullet just a little, letting the aftershock run though her body, releasing another loud moan.

She lays there for a moment, panting, satisfied and lethargic. A few moments later, she is asleep, vibrator still tucked between her thighs, bullet off but resting on her open palm. She lays sprawled naked on the couch, porn still playing on the television.

Chapter Three

Ryan turns off the car in the garage, unplugging his phone and reaching for the bag of food on the front seat. He gets out of the car, then scans the backseat, making sure he hasn't left anything inside. He knows the kids aren't in there, but scanning the car before he leaves is a habit now—one ingrained after he read one too many horror stories about forgetful parents leaving their kids in hot cars when they went to work.

The two car seats occupy the backset, one toddler size for Penny and the base for Oliver's carrier. He takes a moment to think of his children, of how much he loves them, then smirks, loving the idea of an entire weekend without them. He loves being a dad, but he needs alone time with Emily, time for them to be adults, to indulge their appetites. Nodding, he leaves the garage, heading for the door into the kitchen. He puts the paper bag of Italian food on the counter, eyebrow raising as he sees that the dishes from their afternoon snack are still on the counter.

That's weird. Emily is normally a neat freak. For a moment, panic slices through him, fear that something has happened to his clean freak of a wife, but then his eyes land on the pair of panties resting atop a pair of yoga pants on the countertop.

What? He walks around the island, picking them up and bringing them to his nose. Worn. He knows this would be cause for alarm if Emily was any other woman, but he looks at the cleaned space behind the sink on the countertop, imagining his wife's naked body squirming against the cold granite.

A sound breaks into his concentration, then, noise that he has been hearing since he walked inside the house but hasn't quite registered until now. *Is that...?*

He tucks the panties into his pocket, abandoning the food on the counter, and heads down the hallway toward the sound.

"Oh yes!" a woman's voice shrieks. "Fuck me harder!"

Ryan grins. For a second, he wonders if the screaming woman is actually in the living room with his wife.

Best Wife Ever! Ryan imagines what lucky man is fucking the stranger right now, waiting for his chance to fuck Emily next. It wouldn't be the first time his wife has surprised him with a gang bang. Though he enjoys indulging his imagination, he knows he isn't hearing a live sexual encounter. The sound is too perfect, the rhythm too perfect. It's porn on the television. Loud porn.

He walks around the corner into the large room, pausing to appreciate the sight of his wife's naked body sprawled on the couch. A vibrator still nestles between her thighs, but she has turned half on her side, her glorious mane of dark hair spread across her shoulders and back, covering the couch cushion.

The silver bullet in her hand glints in the light from the television, which shows a thin brunette with massive breasts getting pounded from behind by a muscle-bound man while she deep throats the tall man in front of her. The porn star's eye makeup is running down her face, streaking her red cheeks, and sweat coats her curves as she pushes back against the man fucking her.

She pulls off the guy in front of her to glance over her shoulder at him. "Fuck that pussy harder!" she demands. "NOW!" The man grabs her hips and redoubles his efforts, and the woman's silicone breasts jounce in a jagged rhythm as she screams her appreciation, her hand never losing the beat as she strokes the massive cock on the man in front of her.

Skills, Ryan thinks appreciatively. Emily is quite good with both hands, even when suitably distracted by a solid pounding. He pictures the last time he has seen her like that, months ago now, the last time his parents took the kids for a weekend. She'd healed from Oliver and wanted to get back into things with a bang, and Ryan surprised her with a gang bang.

He can still picture it, his beautiful Emily with her head tossed back in ecstasy, mouth eager for the cum to spill over her red lips as she jerked both cocks in front of her, never breaking rhythm, her perfect breasts bouncing as she rode the third man beneath her. She glanced at him seconds before the men exploded on her face, eyes filled with lust and love and satisfaction.

My fucking wife, he thinks again. *I am so fucking lucky.*

She had treated him a few months prior with a lady pile of his own, just before Oliver was born and she was so miserably uncomfortable in pregnancy. She had sprawled on the chaise in the corner of the room, belly huge and eyes filled with glee as she watched him take turns with the women. They had gotten her into the action a little bit, licking her pussy while he fucked them each from behind. She'd been too sensitive for penetration that night, preferring to watch him instead. Near the end of the evening, though, she had been about to come again, mouth frozen in a scream of pleasure, but then she looked over the woman's body right at him, mouthing the words *I fucking love you* right before she exploded in her own orgasm. Ryan hadn't lasted long after that, pumping into the woman and crying out his own pleasure.

We are definitely well suited, he thinks, walking slowly to the couch. He stands there for a moment, watching the porn, feeling himself hardening at the sight and sound. The brunette on screen has shifted her position, now riding one man and tilting forward so the other man can slide into his ass. Ryan smiles, enjoying the sound the woman makes as the cock slowly pushes into her, that deep grunt of satisfaction that a woman only makes when she's got both holes filled. His hand snakes down to his waist, unbuckling his belt and setting it down on the side table. Slipping his hand between the waistband and his belly, he gives himself a few short pumps, enjoying the feel as he lets the visual slide over him.

He shifts his attention from the television, looking down at his wife, eyes scanning her gorgeous body. He's seen her take two men at once, heard her make that sound, but it's been a long time. Glancing at the clock, he decides that tonight, he will hear that noise again. *At least three,* he decides, *definitely one more man, though two would be better, so I can watch her face as she is filled. I want to hear her scream her pleasure. I want to watch her experience every sensation. But for now, a preview...*

He plucks the bullet from her hand, moving gently so he doesn't wake her, not wanting to disturb her yet. Kneeling on the floor in front of the couch, he is careful not to jostle her as he slowly runs a hand up from her foot to her shin, pausing to cup her knee when she moans a little. When she settles again, he continues his motion up her leg, loving the satiny texture of his wife's smooth thighs. When he approaches the apex of her thighs and her still glistening pussy, she moans a little more, shifting her body so his hands have easier access to where her dream-filled body wants him to go.

When she finishes the roll onto her back, Ryan catches the vibrator still between her legs, careful not to hit the button to turn it on. He knows that Emily likes to have just the tip inside of her when he plays with her clit, enjoys the dual sensations of a teasing fullness and ecstatic pleasure. He presses it slowly between her legs, resting the tip against her opening, but not pushing inside, wanting to wait for her to wake a little more and push down when she is ready.

Emily emits another moan, this one more sexy and less sleepy. Ryan leans down, positioning himself between her thighs, and takes a long slow lick from where the vibrator rests against her slit to the top where her clit waits, hard and plump from her earlier sessions. She moans again, a hand drifting down to tangle in his hair, and Ryan focuses his efforts, knowing that she likes to come hard and immediately when she wakes up, none of that slow teasing she enjoys at other times. He bends to his work, tongue pulsing against her clit the way he knows she likes, one hand holding the vibrator in place as she slowly scoots down, the tip just entering her pussy.

"Fuck," she says, the word long and drawn-out in that sultry voice he loves, and he pushes the vibrator up a smidge, just enough to remind her that he is controlling her pleasure this time. "Baby," she moans, shuddering, her other hand coming to rest on his shoulder while she fists his hair, tugging him closer, her hips begin to move, urging him on.

Ryan waits until she is right on the edge, then pushes the button to engage the vibrator, the toy roaring to life inside of her, and Emily shrieks. At the same time, he sucks hard on her clit, knowing that while she enjoys pressure and motion to get her to orgasm, sucking her clit pushes her over the edge. She comes with a scream of delight, body shaking beneath him.

Ryan pauses long enough to let her catch her breath, resting his cheek on her sweat-sticky thigh, enjoying the rosy flush of her skin. When she opens her eyes to looks down at him, finally back into herself again, he moves back to her pussy, licking hard and fast while he moves the vibrator just a tiny bit back and forth, in and out, the tip teasing her sensitive lips, and then she comes again, harder this time, fierce.

"Fuck yeah!" she roars, then uses both hands to tug him up her body. "I need you inside me, Ryan," she breathes into his ear, biting the lobe as her hands drag up and down his back. Ryan fumbles with his pants, unbuckling the button with one hand while shoving them off his hips with the other. He pushes them down one hip, freeing his hard cock, and uses his feet to tug them down the rest of the way as he slides forward, pressing into her core just above the vibrator. The toy still buzzes, the sensation fun against the length of his cock as he rests above it. Emily grabs his shoulder hard, wrapping her legs around his hips to pull him closer while one hand snakes between their bodies to shove the vibrator out of the way. It thumps onto the carpeted floor, the buzz sending it rolling away next to Ryan's knee. He ignores it, plunging his cock into his wife, loving the guttural sound of pleasure that comes out of her as he slides inside.

"Yes!" she screams, almost in time to the porn on the television. Ryan would turn to watch, enjoying the visuals as he fucks his own partner, but the TV is behind him, and he doesn't want to turn around. Looking up, he sees that Emily is watching him, but her eyes flick to the screen every now and then, and he realizes that she is using her legs to adjust his timing to match the sounds coming from the porn. Once he understands her intention, Ryan adjusts immediately, matching his rhythm to the one he can hear behind him, and Emily lets loose a round of moans as she bites his earlobe, digging her nails into his back as she claws him closer with each pounding thrust. "Like that yes!" she screams again, and her pussy tightens around him, waves of pleasure echoing from her into him.

Not yet, he reminds himself. *The night is still young.* He changes his rhythm, and Emily allows it, needing to catch her breath after yet another orgasm so soon, and he kisses her slowly, starting with the ear near his mouth. He moves down, nipping and kissing her neck in soft wet bursts, then curls his back so he can run his tongue down her shoulder to her perky nipples. She sighs, legs tightening around his hips as he takes the first one into his mouth, and he slides his hand between their bodies, swiping across her clit. Emily shudders against him, head tilting back as she bites her lip at the sensation.

"Oh yeah baby," she moans.

Ryan raises his head to look at her, still moving his hips so he continues to fuck her, but slowly now, gently, letting the moment build back up when it will. To distract himself, he thinks of the food he left on the kitchen counter. The chicken parmesan will need to be reheated when they finally pause long enough to remember how hungry they are. He wonders about the fettuccine alfredo—it will probably separate if they use the microwave. He continues to suck her nipple, random thoughts slowing his desire, bringing him away from the edge.

She sighs again, hands tightening their grip on his shoulders, and he looks up at her face. Leaning in for a slow kiss, he lingers on her mouth, hand still pressing gently against her clit as he continues to rock his hips, pressing in and out of her with slow delicious strokes.

Breaking the kiss, he looks at his wife. She is watching him now, eyes dark with lust and sultry with spent passion. She doesn't have many orgasms left before he'll need another break.

"You naughty vixen," he says, "whatever were you doing on our kitchen counter, Mrs. Carter?"

"Me?" she replies, eyes widening in feigned innocence. "What do you mean, Mr. Carter?"

"Did you play with your pussy in the kitchen?" he prompts. "Did you come on the kitchen counter without me?"

"Maybe," she admits. "But I thought of you."

"I'll give you something to think about," he promises. "Did you think about this cock fucking you?"

She nods, biting her lip again as he increases the pace of his thrusts a little, the dirty talk getting him hot as he watches her reactions. "I like thinking about your cock in my pussy," she says with a teasing grin.

"This cock?" he asks, pounding a few hard thrusts to make the point.

"Yes!" she gasps, eyes closing for a second. "That fucking cock!"

"Take my cock," he demands. "Take it all!"

"Yes!" she agrees, tightening her legs around his hips again and lifting herself off the couch a little in her eagerness to be near him. "Fuck me with that hard cock!"

Ryan feels what little time he gained thinking about food slipping away. He's not going to last much longer. "Come for me, baby," he orders. "Come on my hard fucking cock."

"I will!" she says, and he moves even faster, hand abandoning her clit to grip the cushion behind her, using it to balance as his motions become frenzied. Emily's pussy tightens around his cock as he pounds into her, her heels digging into his lower back as she jerks in closer. The sounds of the fucking on the TV are eclipsed by their own noises of hard fucking, wet flesh slamming together. "Yes!" Emily shrieks. Ryan roars as her orgasm vibrates through his cock, and seconds later, he is coming in a rush, flooding into her. He pumps a few more times, eager for every last moment of ecstasy, then collapses forward, breathing hard.

"Baby," he croons a bit later, lifting a sweat-soaked head from her shoulder to kiss her plump lips. "You are so goddamn sexy."

"Did you bring food?" she asks, ever practical.

"I did," he replies. "Italian from Giardino's. Though it's probably cold now."

"You are so sexy when you reheat food," she tells him. "I prefer it when you do it naked."

"It's not bacon, so I wouldn't do it any other way," he says. "Besides, I understand there's a countertop that needs to be utilized."

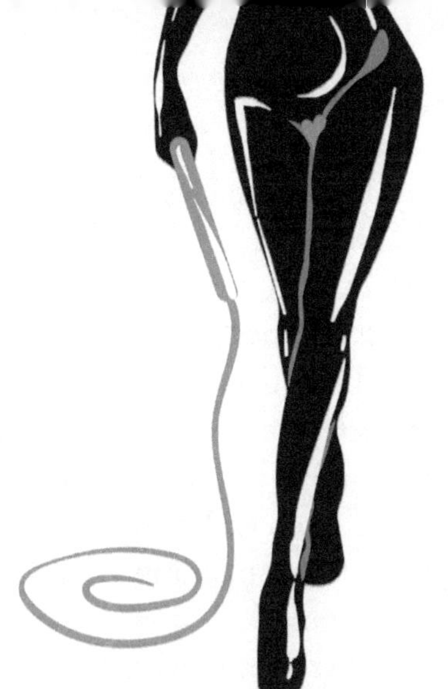

Chapter Four

"There is nothing sexier than a naked man in front of a stove," Emily comments from her perch on the countertop next to the sink. Ryan looks over his shoulder to wink at her, then turns back to the pan of fettuccine alfredo he is attempting to coax back into some semblance of a cream sauce, stirring the noodles. The smell from the oven is intoxicating, warm cheese and chicken and red sauce from the main course teasing both of their senses.

"Except maybe a naked woman with a cock in her mouth," Ryan offers, and Emily laughs, a rich satisfied sound that he always looks forward to on these rare weekends alone. "Just let me get some food in my belly," she says, "and I'll follow it up with a hard cock in no time." She leans over to cut another slice from the bread they already removed from the oven, smearing it with a touch of butter and taking a big bite.

"Don't go filling up on bread," Ryan warns. "I have many more things to put in your mouth tonight."

Emily smiles around her mouthful, playfully giving him the finger behind his back. "Don't ever get between a woman and her carbs," she warns.

Ryan chuckles, lifting the spatula to his chest as he spins to face her. "I don't think this is salvageable," he admits. "But we can still eat it?"

Emily nods, knowing that their encounter in the living room is well worth separated cream sauce and greasy noodles. Ryan steps away, leaning down to open the oven and retrieve the chicken parmesan. He uses the towel instead of a proper pot holder, a habit that is both endearing and frustrating to his wife. Wincing a little, he puts the pan down on the stovetop next to the pan of fettuccine quickly.

"Wet spot on the towel?" she asks, knowing that his habit of using towels to grab hot things has led to more than one burn.

"It's fine," Ryan says, bringing his hand to his mouth, sucking the side of his finger. "No big deal."

"You know there's this wonderful invention called a potholder. It keeps you from burning your fingers on hot things," she snarks at him, leaning over to cut another piece of bread, this one for him.

"Really?" he asks, turning to pull two plates down from the cabinet. He puts the chicken on the plates, then hands her one, grabbing them both forks from the drawer. She puts the newly buttered bread on his plate with a grin, then puts her plate on the counter next to her, leaning down to cut off a bite of chicken. She lifts it to her mouth eagerly, the smell heavenly.

"Mmm," she moans as she chews.

"S'good," Ryan agrees, and she looks up to see him watching her eat as he leans against the counter on the other side of the sink, his back to the stove now. He takes a few bites and chews appreciatively, and there is companionable silence in the kitchen.

When Emily finishes her chicken, she hops off the counter and kneels next to Ryan, who turns to face her with a mouthful of food. "Huh?" he asks, but then she is twisting his hips so he is directly facing her, his semi-erect cock in her face.

"I was promised hard cock after dinner," she says, leaning forward to suck him entirely into her mouth. Ryan grunts, thighs tightening as his hands grip the side of the counter.

"I got us dessert," he mentions a few moments later, obviously an afterthought as Emily continues to suck his cock. "But this is nice too."

He hardens almost immediately in her mouth, his full length filling her mouth and teasing the back of her throat. He swallows a final bite of chicken, then reaches over to where the separated alfredo still sits in the pan on the stove. He grabs a strand of fettuccine, then lowers it in front of Emily's face, making sure it's not hot before draping it over his cock. Without missing a beat, Emily sucks it into her mouth, butter and cream sliding along his cock. She pulls back, her hand picking up where her mouth left off, chewing before she swallows. A wicked grin slips across her lips as she opens her mouth at him, clearly asking for more. Ryan obliges, lifting two strands of fettuccine from the pan. He slides one into her mouth, watching as her luscious lips close over the buttery pasta. He drapes the other over his cock, enjoying the view and the sensation as she sucks that one into her mouth as well, taking him inside just as she swallows, the suction pulling hard. He groans, grabbing another strand, but instead of wrapping it around his cock, he pops it into his mouth. Gesturing for Emily to stand up, he easily lifts her onto the countertop, leaning down to lick her pussy with the buttery pasta still in his mouth. She moans at the slippery feel, and Ryan grins. He reaches into the pan and lifts a small handful, dropping it slowly onto her sensitive skin. Warm pasta and butter drips over her body, and she shivers, leaning up on her shoulders to watch as Ryan slowly begins eating the noodles, sucking and teasing her slit as he pushes the food around, using her as both spoon and plate, catching stray runnels of butter as she squirms beneath him.

"I'm going to need a shower after this," she moans, an eyebrow lifted in his direction.

"Of course," he replies, "You're a dirty fucking girl. You always need a shower."

"But I was looking forward to going out tonight smelling like sex," she teases. "I wanted you to watch me fucking other men knowing that I smell like you." She smirks, eyes closing as he takes a long lick, finishing the remaining pasta and cleaning his "plate." "But now I just smell like Italian food."

"Amazing Italian food," Ryan agrees, taking another taste.

"I thought I was promised dick for dessert," Emily reminds him.

"So demanding," Ryan says, stepping closer to stand between her legs. The counter is the perfect height, the tip of his cock pressing against her opening. "You want a little more cock for dessert?" he asks.

"Please," she says, moving to wrap her legs around his hips and tug him into her. But Ryan moves too fast, slipping out of reach. She pouts at him. "But my dessert!"

Ryan smiles, stepping over to the refrigerator and opening the freezer door. He plucks a piece of ice from the tray and kicks the door shut behind him. "You will have your dessert," he promises, "but right now this is an Italian pussy." He stands over her, letting the ice drip onto her sensitive skin.

She winces as the first drops fall, icy water sliding down her skin, teasing and stimulating. "You don't want Italian pussy?" she breathes.

He rewards her question with a swipe of the ice along her slit, a quick back and forth that has her arching her back and pulling away from him. "I just had Italian food," Ryan tells her. "Now I want my fucking wife's pussy."

"Come and get it," she says, opening her legs wide as she bites her lip, giving him her best sexy eyes.

He swipes the ice again, following the motion with his hands, spreading the water all over her and cutting the grease from the alfredo. "You want this cock?" he asks, pressing himself up against her opening.

"You know it," she says. "Always."

"Tell me," he orders, cold hand running along his cock, fingers pressing against her around the head. "Tell me how you want this cock."

"I want you inside me," Emily croons. "I need you deep in my pussy. Fuck me on this perfect kitchen counter. Claim me before we go out and find more people to fuck. Show me whose pussy this is."

Ryan makes it halfway through her speech before losing control and pushing into her warm heat, letting her pussy envelop him as he slides home. Her legs wrap immediately around his hips and her hands reach out to grip his waist, trying to set the rhythm.

Ryan lets her at first, allowing her to choose their pace and grinning when she picks a vicious tempo, hands jerking his waist hard, so he pounds in and out of her. Ryan sets his feet, leaning forward with one hand gripping to counter to hold himself steady while the other slides beneath her ass, strong fingers pressing her hard against him with each thrust.

"Whose pussy is this?" he demands when she tosses her head back in pleasure, close to losing herself. His other hand abandons the counter and slides up to grip her hair, tugging her head back. She opens her eyes, staring deep into his as she answers him. "Yours!" she yells. "Always yours!"

"I fucking love you!" he says, pounding hard into her. "And I love fucking you!"

"You're my favorite fuck!" she insists. "I love you so fucking hard!"

He feels her begin to climax, her pussy tightening around his cock as she shudders against him, body taut on the countertop. He lets himself go, joining her in release, knowing that the next time he sees her come, it will probably be with someone else. The idea only gets him hotter, and he explodes inside her.

"Best dessert ever," Emily mumbles a few minutes later. Ryan pushes himself up on his elbows from where he collapsed half on top of her. Her legs spasm a few times, muscles worked hard, and he leans down to kiss her tenderly.

"You excited about tonight?" he asks, nuzzling her neck.

"Always," she says. "I can't wait to watch you fuck someone. I want to watch someone come on your cock."

Ryan grins, slowly rising, letting the feeling come back into his legs before he stands, letting go of the countertop. He takes a few steps away on rubbery legs, holding out a hand to help her down. Emily sits up slowly, body still flushed from her orgasms. She takes his hand to hop off the counter, then smirks at him.

"See?" she says, gesturing at the countertop. "Granite is totally worth it."

"Sold," Ryan agrees, smiling at her reference to their discussion when building the house. Ryan had wanted quartz at first. Now he is glad Emily convinced him to go granite.

"Shower?" she asks, glancing at the dishes still littering the counter. "Or dishes first?"

"Shower," Ryan says decisively. "If we spend more time in this kitchen, I'm only going to fuck you again, and by the time we actually get to the club, it will be sunrise, and everyone you want to play with will be asleep."

Emily grins at him, taking a few steps out of the kitchen and through the hall to the stairs. "So, you don't want to fuck on the stairs?" she asks, sashaying her hips as they walk up slowly. Ryan reaches out to swat her ass and she yelps, narrowing her eyes at him. "How about in the bedroom?"

"I was thinking about the shower," Ryan admits, "at least once more before we go."

"Alright," Emily agrees, "But this time I get to be on top."

Chapter Five

When they first walk into the club, Emily and Ryan hold hands, each scanning the space, considering the opportunities of each person inside. The cage to the right of the entrance is occupied: a blonde wearing a pink bra and what look like rubber bands around her thighs is inside, a man fucking her from behind through the bars as she sucks another cock, her hands clearly straining against the restraints, eager to touch, to grip, to pull. Others stand outside, hands stroking between her legs, pinching her nipples, holding her long hair back from her face. A few men stroke their cocks watching the show, ready to cum on her when the time comes.

Emily smiles, knowing that while she enjoys group sex as much as the next girl, she would never be satisfied inside the cage. She needs to be involved in the action. Handcuffed and blindfolded while she receives the attention may be fun for a few moments, but it's not what she craves. She does enjoy watching though, catching the eye of a man who stands on the opposite side of the cage, his fingers deep between the blonde's legs. He watches her for a moment, invitation in his gaze as he continues to rub, and the blonde shudders at the magic he works with his fingers. Emily winks at him, nodding, letting him know she'd like to get to know him better when he finishes with his current partner.

"We're late," Emily comments quietly, seeing the various scenes already underway around the club.

Ryan nuzzles her neck, and she sags into him. "Would you trade the kitchen for earlier scenes?"

Emily shakes her head. "No. Totally worth it." She looks around, considering their options. "And because we're later, there's more to choose from." Sometimes, the club takes a little while to get going, some patrons shy about being the first to get the party started. They have skipped that part of the evening, arriving when everyone is past those initial jitters and fully embracing their sexuality. She glances at Ryan, both of them conspicuously overdressed among the half-naked club members. "This playground is in full swing."

"Can't wait to see you having a good time," Ryan murmurs, his eyes watching the girl in the cage for a few moments before he moves to the next scene. Handcuffs aren't really his thing, though he does enjoy a good blindfold now and then. One of his favorite things to do with Emily in a group setting is to blindfold her and let her guess which cock she's sucking—or holding or fucking. She's quite good at keeping track of everyone. She can tell which pussy she's licking too, though Ryan knows that's not too difficult. Women are different in a way he can't tell with cocks, though he's sucked his fair share. He doesn't mind dick, though he prefers pussy.

Beyond the cage, he spies a man lying flat on a bench, a big-breasted woman with a pixie cut bouncing joyfully on his cock while another petite redhead rides his face. The women face each other, happily kissing as the man services them both. As Ryan watches, cock hardening in his pants, another man strolls up to the redhead riding the face, cock hard and mouth height. Without missing a beat, the redhead takes the cock in hand before tugging the man forward to pull him into her mouth. The pixie continues the motion, licking the other side of the new cock, and both women began sucking him in turns. The man closes his eyes, and Ryan appreciates his muscular chest, his short blonde hair, the sizable cock he shares with the two women.

Catching his wife's eye, Ryan leads Emily to the scene on the bench, watching her reaction as they pause near a couple who stand nearby. The woman wears a dress, like Emily, and her partner has his hands up the bottom, clearly stroking her beneath the red silk. Emily's dress is green, and she bites her lip as she watches the woman's face, her eyes fluttering closed in pleasure and then sliding open to watch the show playing out on the bench. The two women continue to share the blonde's penis while fucking the man beneath them, the pixie reaching down with her free hand to cup the redhead's breast as she presses herself into the man's face. The man on the bench has his hands around the redhead's hips, the only visible part of him a mane of black hair fanning the bench below and the flash of dark hair around his cock as it appears when the pixie lifts herself up.

The woman in the red dress moans, dragging Emily's attention back to the couple next to them, and she catches Ryan's eye. Reading her intention, he releases her hand, watching her approach the couple, moving to stand on the man's left, careful not to block their view of the show on the bench.

"Mind if I join you?" Emily asks them both. The man whispers something in the woman's ear, a hint of a foreign language, and the woman giggles, turning to glance at Emily with a nod.

"By all means," she replies in a heavy accent. "What do you want of me?"

Emily leans in, tracing her mouth and nose along the woman's neck, her face inches away from the man. His shirt has the top few buttons open, but he is still mostly dressed. "I want to make you cum," Emily says to the woman, "while you watch the show." She pauses to address the man. "Would that be alright?"

The man narrows his eyes at Emily, considering her as his hands move faster beneath his partner's dress, eyes skipping from the show before him to the sexy woman at his side. "Would I then be able to make you cum, mademoiselle?" he asks.

Emily glances at Ryan, who nods quickly. "I'd like that," Emily says. "I'm Emily." She gestures at Ryan. "And that's Ryan."

"Emily," the man repeats, "a lovely name for a lovely lady." He looks down at the woman pressed against him, one hand abandoning its motion beneath the dress to cup a breast through red fabric. "How would you make this lovely lady cum?" he asks. "She likes it when you suck her nipples," he offers. "Don't you, Marie?" he coos, sucking on Marie's ear and eliciting a giggle. "I'm Luca."

"I'd love to see those nipples, Luca, if I may," Emily says, and with a nod from Marie, she moves in front of the woman, slowly unhooking the line of buttons that runs up the front of her dress. "I love this dress," Emily comments, tugging free just enough buttons to reveal Marie's red lace bra. She moves so her body isn't blocking the show, seeing how Marie's eyes follow the bodies on the bench. Emily can see her hard nipples peeking through the lace bra, and she reaches out to cup both breasts, a small handful each, then uses her mouth to slide the lace aside and pulls a turgid nipple into her mouth. Marie gasps, and Emily looks up, catching Luca's eye. His hands have returned to rubbing beneath her dress, and they stay there for a while as Emily moves from one nipple to the other.

The sounds from the bench behind her have intensified, and Emily pauses long enough to glance that way. The players have rearranged themselves. The man on the bench, who she now sees is a hottie beneath all that glorious hair, is now fucking the redhead from behind while she kneels on the bench, her face buried in the pixie's pussy. The pixie lays on her back while two cocks take their turns with her mouth, a man standing on either side of the bench. Emily recognizes the man from earlier who shared his cock with both women, but she doesn't recognize the other man, the one whose back is to her. It's a lovely back, toned and covered in swirling tattoos up to his bald head. Emily wants to touch him, to feel that smooth skin against her own. The black-haired god notices her attention and winks at her, a promise for later.

Emily returns her attention to Marie, no longer satisfied with nipples. She needs more. "Marie," she whispers, moving her mouth close to the woman's ear, "I want to taste you."

Marie moans, a hand reaching around to tug Emily's face to hers, soft lips pressing against her mouth. The kiss begins sweetly enough, but quickly turns passionate, Emily and Marie both aroused by the show. As she stands entwined in Marie's arms, Luca wraps his arms around them both, gently cupping Emily's ass through her green dress. She knows he can feel that she isn't wearing panties. Emily slides a hand down Marie's waist, following the line of her thigh before doping beneath the dress. Her fingers encounter Luca's as they slide Marie's panties aside, the man's hand splayed so one finger is inside while his thumb rubs Marie's clit. Emily puts her fingers alongside his thumb and begins rubbing slowly up and down. Luca takes the hint, his thumb retreating, no doubt so he can slide more fingers inside Marie.

Emily knows when he does so because Marie bucks hard, gasping into Emily's mouth at the sensation. Emily continues to kiss her, slow and sensual, her fingers setting a steady rhythm against Marie's clit. The woman begins moaning into her mouth, and Emily knows she is close. When she is right on the edge, Emily breaks the kiss long enough to whisper into her mouth, "Come for me, beauty. Come on my hand."

Marie's eyes open, watching the show over Emily's shoulder and she lets go, the orgasm flooding her. Marie makes a delightful sound, a noise Emily wants to hear again. Luca takes the moment to lean forward and capture Emily's lips with his own, kissing her deep and slow. The hand on her ass creeps slowly around to her thigh, then slides between her legs, long finger brushing against her seam. "So wet," he murmurs. "So lovely."

"You wanted to make me cum?" Emily reminds him, one hand sliding over Marie's breast while the other tangles itself in Luca's hair.

"Oh, yes," Marie says, joining the conversation from between them. "Luca is marvelous with his tongue." She glances to her right, taking in Ryan, the pronounced bulge in his pants as he watches his wife sandwich the couple. "Oh, poor baby," Marie says, slipping out from between them. "Surely, Marie can help with that!" She drops to her knees after a glance at Luca, who nods quickly, eager for the next round to proceed. Ryan grins down at the lovely dark-haired Marie, who licks her lips as she begins unbuttoning his pants. "I hope you taste as sweet as your wife," Marie says.

"Oh yes," Emily promises. "He's delicious." Emily watches as Marie tugs Ryan's cock free, her red lips taking his hard length deep in her throat without a sound. Ryan smiles, hands running through her hair, eyes closed. Luca presses himself against Emily's back, his hands sliding up and down her sides, teasing her as Marie sucks her husband's cock. Ryan opens his eyes after a moment, watching her with Luca before his gaze drifts to the scene on the bench.

The partners have shifted again, and this time, the dark-haired god is standing back, the blonde having taken his position behind the redhead. The bald man is laying on his back on the bench while the pixie slowly rides his cock, facing the redhead who seems to be taking turns licking the pixie's clit and the bald man's balls. As they watch, another man from the sidelines steps up, unbuttoning his pants and holding his cock over the bald man's face. There is a momentary pause as the bald man gets his bearings, and then his tongue is licking the new length, hands reaching up to stroke as he cups the balls.

Emily looks beyond the scene to meet the dark-haired man's gaze again. He is watching her as Luca slides his hands over her body, eyes filled with promise. His cock, which had been flagging after cumming with the redhead, seems to be jerking slowly back to life. His hand strokes himself idly, watching her. He glances at the bench and the women who seem very occupied, then makes his way over to where Emily and Luca stand.

"Can I join you?" he asks, his voice a low rumble that does things deep inside Emily's core.

"Please," she says, and Luca's hands slide over her dress to cup her breasts. He nuzzles her neck, muttering foreign endearments, and Emily smiles deep and warm, liquid heat pooling in her center.

"This is Emily," Luca introduces. "She is deliciously wet."

The big man smiles. "I'm Carter," he says, "and I want to taste your cunt. Can I lick your sweet pussy, Emily?"

"Oh yes," Emily agrees. "That would be wonderful."

Carter kneels before her, and Emily sinks back into Luca's embrace, reveling in the strong man behind him and the novelty of the hulking man on his knees before her. Luca begins tugging her dress up an inch at a time, while Carter slides his huge hands up the outside of her legs, following the lifting material. When the dress is nearly to her waist, Carter says, "Show me that sweet pussy, Emily."

Luca obliges, lifting the material up to reveal her smooth skin. Carter leans forward, both hands sliding inward to stroke her flesh. Emily shivers, and Luca continues to kiss her neck, her ears, occasionally catching her mouth as she turns to meet him. As Luca's lips meet hers, Carter presses his mouth against her lower lips, and Emily moans into Luca's mouth. Luca curses as she presses hard against him, a soft sound in another language. She can feel the bulge of his erection behind her, pressing against her ass as Carter pushes her back with the force of his tongue and mouth.

She shivers against him, and Carter pauses, looking up at her. "Sweet pussy indeed," he says. "I want you to cum on my face, Emily." His finger strokes the seam of her pussy, teasing, promising, and then his finger is dipping just inside, a tiny bit, just the way she likes it. She manages to look up and sees that the pixie from the bench has joined Marie with Ryan, the two women tugging his shirt over his head as they lead him not to the bench, but to a low wide leather table in a corner of the club. She watches him as he sits on the edge, Marie quickly settling herself between his legs to continue sucking his cock while the pixie presses her body against his bare back, leaning around to kiss him. Emily loves to watch Ryan kiss other women. She knows what his mouth can do.

The mouth between her legs has grown more insistent, and Emily gasps as both of her legs are suddenly lifted to rest atop Carter's shoulders, the man settling himself to his work with dedication. She grabs his head with one hand, relishing the feel of that glorious mane under his fingers while her other hand still holds Luca's shoulder. The other man holds her upper body easily, still caressing her breasts as he kisses her neck. The orgasm is quick and hard, sudden as Carter's fingers find a magic spot inside that causes her to unravel in his arms.

Emily is still floating in pleasure as Luca and Carter carry her to the table next to Ryan. Carter lifts her dress over her head, and she reaches forward to unbutton Luca's pants. His cock pops out immediately, long and lean. Ryan sits next to her, Marie between his legs and the pixie still behind him, but as Emily joins them, the pixie leans down to kiss her.

Emily can taste Ryan on her lips, and while her hands still reach to caress Luca's cock, she lingers in the kiss. More hands grip her hips, Carter kneeling behind her and leaning down to kiss her neck. The pixie breaks off the kiss to lean behind and kiss Carter, the two sharing a hungry look. Ryan uses the pause to kiss his wife, a hand reaching up and behind him to cup the pixie's breast while she kisses Carter. Luca leans over just enough to swat Marie's ass. She squeals, leaving Ryan's cock long enough to look at her partner with hooded eyes.

"I want to fuck this cock," Marie says. "May I?" Her gaze swivels from Luca's nod over to Emily.

Emily nods. "Please," she says. "It's an amazing cock."

"I'm going to sit on your face," the pixie says to Ryan while staring at Carter. "Lean back."

Ryan obliges, settling himself on the surface as the two women clamber over him. Emily watches the satisfaction on Marie's face as she slides onto his cock. Once atop him, she tugs her red dress overhead, though she leaves her red bra and panties on, sliding the material aside so she can fuck Ryan. The pixie watches for a moment, leaning over to kiss Marie as she begins to move slowly, then kneels over Ryan's face. Emily watches his tongue dart out to lick her, and heat pools in her middle again.

Luca is standing in front of her, and she turns her attention back to the lovely cock in front of her face. She takes him in her mouth eagerly, enjoying the smooth skin against her tongue. Carter is behind her, his cock fully hard once again, pressing against her back. "Let me have your pussy," Carter orders. "Let me inside you." Emily twists, getting on her knees, her hand still stroking Luca in front of her. "I want you to watch me fucking you," Carter says in that deep voice, and Emily turns her head, not sure how to accommodate him. "Turn around, beauty," Carter says. Emily spins again, this time putting her legs toward Carter while her face stays near Luca. She props herself up on her elbows, Luca's cock sliding along her lips as she looks down the length of her body to watch as Carter kneels before her, big arms sliding her hips up to meet him. He pauses, dragging out the moment, letting the head of his cock rest against her opening as he stares at her face. Her mouth opens, eager for Luca's cock between her lips, and her eyes glance over to watch Marie riding Ryan, her husband's face still buried in the pixie's pussy.

"I want you to watch," Carter says, "and I think you want him to watch." He reaches over to tap the pixie, who opens her eyes. Seeing the expression on Carter's face, she smirks, climbing off Ryan and kneeling beside him. Ryan turns to watch Emily and she smiles at him as Carter presses his huge cock into her, stretching her.

"Oh fuck," she groans, "that's good!"

"You like that, beauty?" Carter asks, one hand gripping her hip hard as he tugs her back into him, the other reaching over to pinch the pixie's breast.

"Oh yeah," Emily moans, refocusing her attention on Luca's cock in front of her face. As she watches, Marie rides herself to a glorious climax, helped along by the pixie's fingers on her nipples. She pauses to catch her breath, climbing off Ryan, and the three rearrange themselves so Ryan can fuck the pixie instead. Emily enjoys watching the muscles of his back as he pounds into the pixie, the woman's face clenching in obvious pleasure as her husband finds the rhythm she wants.

Carter listens to the sounds of the pixie with Ryan for a moment, slowly fucking Emily as they both watch the show, but when the pixie cries out her release, Carter turns back to his work, serious now as he pushes into Emily. She normally can focus on two dicks at once, but the huge cock is too much, and soon she has forgotten Luca completely, both hands clinging to Carter's hips as he pounds into her.

"Come on my dick!" he demands, the words making her fly over the edge as she obeys, watching his cock pound into her.

"Again?" he asks a moment later when she returns to herself. When she nods, he leans down to kiss her, and she can taste herself on his lips. Perhaps the pixie too. She remembers the way he buried his face in her pussy and shudders again, a small climax echoing through her.

"I want..." she begins, still catching her breath. "I want to sit on your face again."

Carter chuckles, a deep masculine sound, and he leans back. Emily pauses for a moment, then considers Luca behind her. "And... I want him to fuck me while you lick my pussy."

Carter glances back at Luca, the two men having a silent conversation, then the big man shrugs and gestures for her to slide up his body. Luca follows, his pants abandoned on the floor beside the table, climbing over Carter. He sheds his shirt as he settles himself behind her. His chest is pale and lean, but with faint lines of muscle—*very European swimmer*, she thinks.

Emily puts a knee on either side of Carter's head, and his tongue reaches out to lick her clit. She moans, sinking into him. A moment later, she feels the press of Luca's cock against her opening, and she shifts her weight slightly to adjust the angle. Luca is long and lean, and he slides into her easily, groaning as he does, pressing his chest against her back, hands reaching around to cup her breasts.

"Oh!" the pixie says from Emily's left. "I see a free cock!" She moves, climbing atop Carter behind Luca, sheathing his cock inside of her as she leans forward, caressing Luca's balls from behind him.

"I think we can manage a little train!" Luca says, pushing slowly back and forth inside Emily. She giggles, knowing that he's not using the right word for their position, but loving his accent and enthusiasm. Carter's mouth continues to work magic on her clit, Luca's cock hitting the perfect spot, and soon she is crying her pleasure, body shuddering atop Carter's face. Her legs give out for a moment, but it doesn't matter; Carter is easily able to support her weight with his hands. She sags back against Luca, and Carter moves her to sit on his chest instead. The pixie makes a noise from behind them, and Emily glances over in time to see him crawling over to where Ryan and Marie are frantically fucking, both of them lost in the moment.

Emily watches Marie's face as she cums hard, the red flush of her skin beneath the sheen of sweat.

"Come with me, *ma petite*," Luca croons in her ear. "I want your sweet ass." Emily turns her head to look at him, her mouth finding his as he moves a few more times, cock still hard inside her. "But can you take us both?" Luca asks, lifting her back as they scoot down Carter's body. Luca lifts her off his cock and slides her onto Carter instead. She sighs as Carter fills her, then bites her lip as Luca pushes her forward, her breasts swinging into Carter's waiting hands. The dark-haired man leans up to catch her mouth, kissing her deeply as

Luca slides his cock against her asshole. She groans at the pressure, losing herself in the sensation of Carter's cock deep inside her, his mouth against hers, the slow gentle intrusion of Luca's cock in her ass. When the smaller man has seated himself, he pulls back slowly, the sensation of both cocks inside of her enough to make Emily's eyes roll back in ecstasy. She begins to cum almost immediately as the men slowly move, keeping an opposite rhythm, so as one cock retreats, the other fills her.

"Oh yes," she moans, riding the wave of pleasure. When she opens her eyes, Ryan is staring at her, eyes dark with heat as he fucks the pixie from behind while she buries her face in Marie's pussy. Emily's orgasm only grows deeper, stronger, and as she feels it begin to sweep her away, she mouths to Ryan, *I fucking love you.*

I love you, he mouths, and then his head tilts back as he lets himself go, flooding the pixie with cum. As if Ryan's yell is the signal, both men inside Emily let go as well, filling her with warmth. She shudders on their cocks, soaking in the aftershocks as she watches Marie cum again on the pixie's talented tongue.

After a moment, Luca slides out of her ass. Carter lifts her gently and settles her beside him. Emily is vaguely aware of the others moving slowly, curling up against the nearest body to catch their breath.

Luca snuggles up on her other side, kissing her neck as his hand rests on one breast. "We must do this again sometime, Mademoiselle Emily," he says. "You must come see us back home and meet our friends."

"Definitely," Emily agrees, meeting Ryan's gaze across the pile. She wonders if his parents would watch the kids for a week while they took an international vacation. "We love exploring new playgrounds."

HONEY POT COLLECTION

Honey Pot Series

Ali Whippe

Ali Whippe

Ali Whippe loves trying new delights, especially of the non-vanilla variety. Her obsession with naughty words and sexy situations is only topped by her need to push the boundaries in every possible way. While her XTC and Honey Pot series play with all things wicked and sultry, the Collectors series is her first foray into paranormal erotica, and she never knew the world of magic and fantasy could be so deliciously sinful. She hopes you enjoy the ride as much as she did.

More Books by Ali Whippe

Office Hours
Tutoring Center
Athletics
Extra Credit
XTC College Series Collection

Swingers

Discovered

Bound for Release
Fetish Circuit
Now You See Me
Sexual Playground

Discover more at
4HorsemenPublications.com

10% off using HORSEMEN10

www.ingramcontent.com/pod-product-compliance
Lightning Source LLC
Chambersburg PA
CBHW020151120726
47903CB00007B/2505

* 9 7 8 1 6 4 4 5 0 7 7 9 7 *